"And what are your Christmas dreams?"

Marshall strained for her answer. But Ainsley shook her head.

"They don't matter. I take life one dream at a time. I'm glad to be here with the babies. And after Christmas my real dreams will begin. I want the job in the ICU. Then, hopefully, I'll get into the nursing program. Everything else is icing on one of these gingerbread cookies."

Why he felt let down, he couldn't say. Maybe he'd hoped he could play a small part in her Christmas dreams.

"And now I get to ask if you have any Christmas dreams of your own." Her face glowed.

"Well, I would like to sneak one of those cookies after we ice them."

She laughed, the sound joyous and tinkling. "I think I can arrange that."

Spending the afternoon and evening with Ainsley was all the Christmas dream he needed. Dreams never worked out all that great for him anyhow. But if he did have one, it would be for this time with Ainsley to last.

Wanting more was a dangerous thing.

Jill Kemerer writes novels with love, humor and faith. Besides spoiling her minidachshund and keeping up with her busy kids, Jill reads stacks of books, lives for her morning coffee and gushes over fluffy animals. She resides in Ohio with her husband and two children. Jill loves connecting with readers, so please visit her website, jillkemerer.com, or contact her at PO Box 2802, Whitehouse, OH 43571.

Books by Jill Kemerer

Love Inspired

Wyoming Cowboys

The Rancher's Mistletoe Bride
Reunited with the Bull Rider
Wyoming Christmas Quadruplets

Small-Town Bachelor
Unexpected Family
Her Small-Town Romance
Yuletide Redemption
Hometown Hero's Redemption

Wyoming Christmas Quadruplets

Jill Kemerer

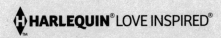

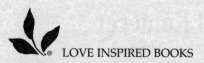

LOVE INSPIRED BOOKS

PLEASE RECYCLE
THIS PRODUCT IS RECYCLABLE

Recycling programs
for this product may
not exist in your area.

ISBN-13: 978-1-335-42838-7

Wyoming Christmas Quadruplets

Copyright © 2018 by Ripple Effect Press, LLC

All rights reserved. Except for use in any review, the reproduction
or utilization of this work in whole or in part in any form by any
electronic, mechanical or other means, now known or hereafter
invented, including xerography, photocopying and recording, or in
any information storage or retrieval system, is forbidden without
the written permission of the editorial office, Love Inspired Books,
195 Broadway, New York, NY 10007 U.S.A.

This is a work of fiction. Names, characters, places and incidents are
either the product of the author's imagination or are used fictitiously, and
any resemblance to actual persons, living or dead, business establishments,
events or locales is entirely coincidental.

This edition published by arrangement with Love Inspired Books.

® and TM are trademarks of Love Inspired Books, used under license.
Trademarks indicated with ® are registered in the United States Patent
and Trademark Office, the Canadian Intellectual Property Office and in
other countries.

www.Harlequin.com

Printed in U.S.A.

The Lord thy God in the midst of thee is mighty;
he will save, he will rejoice over thee with joy;
he will rest in his love, he will joy over thee
with singing.
—*Zephaniah* 3:17

For all the parents and caregivers of multiples.
May you be blessed.

Chapter One

"Belle, would you get the door?" Marshall Graham held Ben in one arm and Max in the other. Both infants were crying as if they hadn't eaten in hours. He'd tried to give them bottles fifteen minutes ago, but Ben had barely touched his, and Max hadn't taken an ounce. The knocking on the front door persisted. "Belle!"

Grace joined in the chorus of wails. *Great.* Marshall glanced at the twin girls strapped in bouncy seats on the living room floor. *Not you, too, Lila.* So far, the most laid-back of the quadruplets merely blinked and shifted her tiny feet. *Thank You, God, for one calm baby. Throw me some mercy with the other three. I'm drowning here.*

The temperature in their remote part of Wyoming had dropped overnight, and if the baby nurse was outside, he'd better get her indoors before she changed her mind about taking the job. Since Belle hadn't stirred from her room, Marshall debated what to do. Set the twins down? Attempt to answer the door? The wind howled, the crying became more urgent and his heart pounded like wild horses across the prairie. Before last week he'd never taken care of even one baby, let alone four.

He was terrible at this.

Gently bouncing both boys in an attempt to soothe them, he hurried to the entrance. Shifting Ben, Marshall unlocked the door and opened it.

The young woman standing on the doormat had sparkling green-gold eyes and a heart-shaped face. A red stocking cap topped with a pom-pom covered her long honey-blond hair. She smiled, and he did a double take. He hadn't expected such an attractive woman to show up. The ratcheting cries didn't let him linger on her appearance, though.

"Come in." Marshall stepped aside for her to hang up her coat. "Follow me."

He hurried to the open-concept living area, then looked down at the boys, their faces screwed up in distress. Now what? He was as close to surrender as he'd ever been.

"Let me." Her soothing voice held authority. She took Max from him and made cooing noises. The baby calmed immediately, staring at her with one teardrop hanging from the outer edge of his eyelashes. "Aw, he's precious. So tiny and sweet."

Tiny, sweet and completely beyond him.

"Oh, you are a darling, aren't you?" She cradled him and turned to Marshall, her eyes glowing with compassion. "I'm Ainsley Draper."

"Marshall Graham." He nodded gruffly. Ben was still crying, and Grace was, as well. Indecision made him hesitate. Did he pick up Grace? Or set Ben down so he could prepare more bottles? Were the babies even hungry? Did any of them need to be changed? Burped? Rocked? Anxiety gripped his torso, tying him in knots.

With Max in her arms, Ainsley carefully lowered herself to kneel in front of the girls. She made silly, kissy faces at them. Grace quieted, her tiny lips wobbling as she watched Ainsley. "Where is your wife?"

Wife? It had been years since he'd had a girlfriend, and he'd never had a wife.

"I'm not married." Marshall placed Ben in a bouncy seat and locked the strap. The baby arched his back and cried louder. "These are my nieces and nephews. I'm helping my twin sister, Belle, and her husband, Raleigh, adjust to life with quadruplets."

Adjust was one way of putting it. Ever since Belle had given birth to the two sets of identical twins five weeks ago, Marshall had been trying to help her any way he could. It was the least he could do given their miserable childhood. Although the quads had been home from the hospital for only a week, he was *this* close to running out to the barns and telling Raleigh it was his turn to deal with the infants. Marshall would rather check cattle for hours on end than change another diaper, which was saying something considering he didn't relish his duties as a cowboy.

For the umpteenth time he wondered if his best friends, Clint, Nash and Wade, were right—maybe he shouldn't be working as a ranch hand for Belle's husband.

But memories rushed back of him and Belle when they were thirteen and fighting off abuse from their mother's latest live-in boyfriend. Marshall had tried to stand up for Belle...and look where it had gotten him.

Separated from his twin. Sent to a group home for boys. Unable to protect Belle from that man.

He would never, ever let his sister down again.

"Oh, so you're just here for a few days or something?" She moved Max to her other arm and turned Ben's bouncy seat so he could face the girls. She began talking to Ben in a low, melodic voice. His crying ceased, followed by a pitiful sigh and a hiccup.

"How did you do that?" Marshall's arms dropped to his sides as he stared at the back of Ainsley's golden hair. She'd been there for—what, three minutes?—and she'd already quieted all four babies.

He suddenly understood the meaning of *baby whisperer.*

She peeked back over her shoulder at him. "Do what?"

"Get them to stop crying. I don't think the house has been this quiet in a week."

She laughed, the sound filling the air with tinkling joy. "I've been babysitting since I was twelve, and I worked at a day care center for years. I have a lot of experience. I will say quadruplets are a first for me, though."

"For me, too."

A flash of understanding passed between them, and he got lost in her pretty eyes. All the tension of being thrust into the role of babysitter dissolved. Help had arrived. He didn't have to do this alone anymore.

He gestured to the kitchen. "I'll get the bottles."

"Is it time to feed them?" She'd turned back to the babies and was strapping Max in the fourth bouncy seat.

"I don't know. What do you mean?"

"Are they on a schedule? When was the last time they ate?"

"I feed them constantly, but they barely eat anything, if that makes sense. All I do is prep bottles and try to feed them, then another fusses, and it's just…" He didn't bother finishing. He'd always considered himself self-reliant, but the past days had driven him to his limit.

"The sooner we get them on a schedule, the better. I'm assuming their mother is resting?"

Belle was resting all right. And avoiding her children along with the real world. He pinched the bridge of his nose. That wasn't fair. She was recovering from their births and needed extra help and a lot of patience.

"Why don't you get the bottles and then tell me their names? We'll feed them together."

Relief jolted through him. He loped to the kitchen and measured out the formula. When the bottles were ready, he tightened both hands around all four and returned to the living room. Ainsley had wrapped Lila and Grace in lightweight blankets. A pastel baby quilt was spread out between the couches, and Ainsley had propped each girl on the infant support pillows he'd never figured out what to do with. All the babies were getting fussy by the time she swaddled Ben.

"Go ahead and feed the girls." Holding Ben,

she took the other two infant support pillows out of the pile of baby paraphernalia in the corner. Within a few minutes, all four babies were snuggled on the floor, happily eating. Marshall held the girls' bottles while Ainsley held the boys'.

"I can't believe it." He glanced at Ainsley, sitting a few feet from him on the floor. "They're all eating at the same time. None of them are crying."

"Yeah, isn't it great?" She grinned. "They're so itty-bitty. Tell me about them. What are their names? Are there any health problems I should know about?"

"They're all healthy. Each one weighs around six and a half pounds, except for Lila. She's the smallest of the bunch." He pointed to one of the girls. "By the way, this one's Lila." He continued down the row. "Grace is here. That's Ben. And Max is next to him."

"How do you tell them apart?"

Heat rushed up his neck. His method was probably stupid.

"Don't laugh, but every morning I mark Grace's pinkie nail with a Sharpie. And I mark Max's with one, too. It's simple to tell the boys from the girls."

She chuckled. "Smart. I would have done the same, except I would have used nail polish."

"Nail polish might be better. I have to reapply the marker often."

"Well, I'm sure these sweethearts will be napping before we know it. Then you can introduce me to your sister, and she can go over the babies' care with me."

He tried not to grimace. He supposed her reaction was normal. Of course a baby nurse would expect the mother to go over the infants' needs with her. But Belle had barely lifted a finger to deal with the children since they'd come home from the hospital last week. If Ainsley was looking for guidance from his sister, she was going to be disappointed. He hoped Belle didn't make a scene. If Ainsley left, he didn't know what he would do.

She'd been there for two hours and still hadn't caught sight of the babies' parents. Was Marshall the only one taking care of them?

Ainsley carried Max and Ben down a hallway to a bedroom with four white cribs. Marshall held the sleeping girls and carefully set them in the same crib. He hitched his chin for her to put the boys into one with navy sheets. When she'd gotten them settled, she tiptoed out of the room with Marshall at her heels.

Her initial plan of meeting the mother and father, going over the babies' schedules and getting a tour of the place before crashing in her room for a while clearly wasn't happening. The long drive from Laramie had wiped her out, but she'd be able to rest later. She hoped so, at least.

She made her way to the living room, swiping up empty bottles and taking them to the kitchen. The sink overflowed with dirty dishes. Half-filled baby bottles littered the counter. A canister of baby formula powder with the cover off was next to the coffeemaker.

"Uh, sorry it's such a mess." Marshall slapped the formula cover on, then opened the dishwasher and unloaded the top shelf. "Been chaotic around here."

"I'm sure." Maybe she was overreacting about not meeting the actual parents. His sister might have had complications from the birth. Now wasn't the time to make snap judgments. She'd simply do her best to figure out what was going on. "So it sounds like you've been really hands-on with the quads. Is their mother having a hard time with recovery?"

"Um, I guess." He didn't look her way as he shoved dirty plates into the dishwasher. "I don't know much about that stuff."

No, the gorgeous cowboy in front of her couldn't be expected to know about recovering from birth, could he? His formfitting black T-shirt had a drip of spit-up on the sleeve. A belt buckle with a tractor on it kept his jeans in place. She could easily picture a cowboy hat on top of his short dark hair. She wasn't sure if his stubble was the result of not having time to shave or if he kept it that way on purpose. Either way, it added to his appeal. Or maybe the fact he'd been holding two tiny babies when he'd opened the door earlier made him a solid ten in her eyes.

A man who protected the helpless was an attractive man indeed.

If Marshall had told her he was the quadruplets' father, she would have quit. It wouldn't be fair to the babies' mother or father to have a nurse who had the hots for their daddy. But since he was their uncle and single, she could stay with no guilt on her conscience. It wasn't as if she was looking for romance, anyhow. After Christmas her sole focus would be on going back to Laramie, getting into the nursing program and finishing her degree.

"How long do they usually nap?" She peered around for the typical infant supplies. No clean bottles were lined up. She didn't see a container with nipples or pacifiers. Where were the bottle brushes?

"Nap?" He finished loading the dishwasher, popped in a cleaning tab and pressed the start button. "They don't usually sleep at the same time."

"What do you mean?" She circled him to get

to the sink and began filling it with hot water. Unscrewing the bottles, she dumped out the old formula into the adjoining basin before tossing them into the soapy water.

"It depends on when they're eating. It's like if one is sleeping, another is hungry."

She checked under the sink for cleaning supplies. A bottle brush and a package of rubber gloves hid behind the dish soap. She slid on a pair of gloves and began washing the bottles.

"How does your sister manage them?"

"Belle?" He wiped his hands on a towel and leaned against the counter. "She's been real tired."

She rinsed the first bottle and looked around for a place to set it. "Do you have a bottle dryer? Or dish towel?"

"Yes. Here." He flicked open a drawer and grabbed two dish towels. Slung one over his arm and spread out the other next to the sink. "I'll take that. If you wash, I'll rinse."

"What about their father? Does anyone else come in to help? A night nurse? Grandmother? Anyone?"

She watched him out of the corner of her eye. The muscle in his cheek leaped.

"No, Raleigh is busy. I wish his mother could have been here to help with the little ones, but she died last year. He inherited Dushane Ranch and has his hands full keeping it going, so he can't be in here all day with the babies. And Belle and I don't have a mother anymore. That's why I hired you."

He hired her? "I thought the babies' parents hired me."

"They'll be glad you're here. When Dottie Lavert told me she knew someone who might be willing to help for a while, I asked her to contact you."

"Dottie made it sound as if your sister— Belle—wanted me to come." A sense of foreboding spilled over her. If neither parent was stepping up to their responsibilities for these babies, Ainsley could be put in a no-win situation. "I don't want Belle resenting me."

"She won't. Look, Belle was desperate for these children. She's going through a rough patch, but she'll be thankful to have you helping with them." He rinsed the bottles and placed them on the towel to dry.

Somehow, Ainsley wasn't so sure. Something didn't seem quite right on Dushane Ranch.

"So let me make sure I've got this straight." She washed the final bottle. "You're taking care of the babies pretty much by yourself?"

"I wouldn't say that. I'm taking a break from my ranch duties to be here during the day. Belle and Raleigh handle the babies at night." His eyes shifted to the side. Was he lying? And what did he mean by taking a break from his ranch duties?

She let the water out of the sink. "I'm sure your sister and her husband will tell me the system that works for them."

"I don't think they have a system." He cleared his throat. "I come over in the wee hours once in a while if Belle texts me."

"Wait, I'm confused. Where do you live?"

He pointed out the kitchen window, which showed views of frozen pastures and distant mountains. "In the second cabin. Right next to yours."

"You work here?" She hadn't expected him to be employed on the ranch. He nodded, but he didn't look very happy about it. She tried to shake her thoughts into some sort of order. Grabbing the dishcloth, she wiped down the counters.

"Yeah," he said. "For now."

"What do you mean?"

Color rose to his cheeks. "Nothing. I'll be here for as long as Belle needs me."

"Well, we'd better get on the same page with these babies. You know I'm only here until after the holidays, right?"

His rich brown eyes looked sheepish. "Until New Year's Eve. We've got you for just over six weeks."

She almost grunted. He wouldn't have her for

even one week if she sensed dysfunction. Growing up with an alcoholic father had soured her on trying to fix other people's problems. How many times had she tried to save her dad from himself? Too many. Worse, she'd put her own life and dreams on hold for years. And what had it gotten her?

Nothing.

That's why she relied on herself. If she found a man who put her first and kept his word, she might be interested in starting a family someday, but finding a guy like that was a tall order.

The best thing she'd ever done was wash her hands clean of her father and his addiction. Three years ago she'd moved to Laramie and enrolled in the University of Wyoming to become a nurse. She'd finished her first two years of schooling, but she was still waiting to get into the highly competitive nursing program. Her college adviser had informed her of a position opening at the hospital in January, which would greatly increase her chances of getting accepted.

Ainsley had already applied for the job. She'd find out in a few weeks if she got it or not. In the meantime, working as a baby nurse would pay her bills and, hopefully, help her get one of the coveted spots in the program.

Marshall waved for them to go back to the

living room. She sat on one of the couches. He sat on the other.

"I don't want you thinking you're here under false pretenses." His knees were wide, and his elbows rested on them. "I've got a cabin ready for you, so you'll have your privacy. The hours are long, but you'll only be on days. No nights. Can you be here from eight in the morning until six?"

"Will I be taking care of the quadruplets all by myself?"

"No, I'll help, too."

Him? But what about their mother?

"Don't you think Belle should be involved?" she asked. Six weeks would pass in a blink, and it would be better if Belle was as hands-on as possible. Ideally, Raleigh would be changing diapers and feeding babies during the day, too, but given his ranch duties, she doubted he'd have time. Hopefully when Ainsley left, Belle wouldn't be overwhelmed trying to care for the children on her own.

"Yes, she should, and if all goes according to plan, I can resume helping Raleigh outside soon."

Nothing ever went according to plan, not in her life, at least. That's why she didn't leave anything she *could* control to chance. As far as this situation went, she might as well take charge now.

"I suggest we color-code these babies. I've

got stickers and markers in my car. I'm going to need you to show me where everything— bottles, bibs, diapers—is stored. When I arrive each morning, I'll make up bottles for the next twenty-four hours and put them in the fridge. All we'll have to do is warm them up. And we're keeping track of how much and when each baby eats. Don't worry. I have charts."

A sense of empowerment rushed up her spine. Maybe she'd been looking at this all wrong. Instead of seeing the potential pitfalls—like four tiny infants and an absent mother and father— she'd focus on the pluses. No system? No problem. She'd impose her own methods on the quadruplets. She'd get them on a schedule.

When Ainsley left, Belle would be comfortable caring for her babies. A surge of purpose filled her chest.

A shuffling sound came from the hallway.

"What is going on?" A beautiful woman with flashing brown eyes and a mane of long black hair appeared in the archway. "Why is this stranger in my living room, Marshall?"

Just when he'd been concentrating on the delicious phrases of *color-code these babies* and *don't worry I have charts*, his sister had to go and kill his good mood. He'd told her he was hiring a baby nurse. He'd gotten Raleigh's approval, too.

"This is Ainsley Draper, the baby nurse we hired. Ainsley, this is my sister, Belle Dushane." He held his breath, waiting to see how Belle would react. His twinstincts told him not well.

"Your babies are beautiful." Ainsley sailed across the room to shake Belle's hand. Her smile brightened the atmosphere. "It's so nice to meet you."

Belle regarded her with distaste and limply shook her hand. Glaring at his sister, Marshall clenched his jaw. She merely raised an eyebrow. He'd always wished he could do the same. His sister certainly had the haughty gesture down pat.

"We don't need a baby nurse." Belle made a shooing motion. "So thank you for coming, but—"

One of the babies let out a cry. Marshall rubbed his temples. *Here we go again.*

Ainsley gestured to the hallway. "Since I'm here, do you want me to stay awhile and help change them?"

Belle's face flushed. "Marshall and I can do it."

Was his sister crazy? Did she honestly think they were in any way succeeding at taking care of quadruplets? They were in way over their heads.

"I understand." Ainsley slowly turned to leave.

"Ainsley, wait." Marshall thrust his hand out. "Stay for a while. We'll sort this out."

Belle snapped her fingers at him. "Come on."

That did it. His sister had crossed many lines lately, and he'd had enough. One of the other babies joined in with the crying. His head began to throb.

"No, Belle." He widened his stance and crossed his arms over his chest. "Don't snap your fingers at me. And don't even think about sending Ainsley away. We need help."

Her chin inclined, and her eyes glinted. "I don't need *anyone* taking care of my babies." Tossing her hair over her shoulder, she stormed down the hall. Marshall debated whether to follow her. If he hadn't shared a womb with her, he'd be tempted to run out the door.

"Should I talk to her?" Ainsley's confused face eased his tension. She didn't seem horrified by his sister's behavior, although he certainly was.

"No, I'll handle it." He entered the babies' room, and his annoyance vanished. Silent sobs racked Belle's back as she stood with her face in her hands over the girls' crib.

"What's wrong?" The girls were crying, too, but he figured they could wait.

"I don't know which one is which, Marsh. I don't know my own babies." She stared up at him with those eyes that had pleaded with him so many times over the years to *fix it*, and he muttered under his breath.

"We're going to change that." With his finger, he raised her chin to look at him. "Four infants are a lot. And I can't do this all by myself, Belle. I know you don't feel well. I don't expect you to be some superwoman. But I'm clueless—I don't know what I'm doing. Ainsley is good with the babies, so let her stay."

He picked up one of the girls. "Here's Lila. The one with the black pinkie nail is Grace. Let's change them."

She swallowed, looking as if she faced a rattler instead of a baby.

He took Grace to one of the changing tables and began unsnapping her coverall. "Who's the prettiest little cowgirl this side of Sweet Dreams, Wyoming?" He cooed. "You're going to break hearts, darlin'." When he'd finished, he picked her back up and turned to see how Belle was doing with Lila. She wasn't in the room. He checked the crib. Lila wasn't either.

He held Grace to his chest and returned to

the living room, hanging back at the sight before him. Belle was handing the baby to Ainsley.

"I'm not feeling well." Belle's face was pinched. "I'm sorry I was rude earlier. Of course we want you to stay."

Ainsley's eyes widened, but she nodded and took the baby. "Why don't you tell me what your expectations are? I want us to be on the same page with their care. I did some research before driving here, and I'd like to use a color system to help manage them."

Belle fidgeted with her wedding ring. "Yes, the color thing sounds good."

"Sit with me?" Shifting Lila to her other arm, Ainsley patted the couch. "Tell me about the babies. What are their personalities like? Should I be concerned about anything?"

Belle's throat worked. She shook her head. "I… I don't feel well. We'll talk later." Then she spun and fled past Marshall down the hallway to her bedroom.

He exhaled, his cheeks puffing out. At least she'd apologized to Ainsley. But what if the damage had been done? Was the apology enough to make Ainsley stay?

"I'm sorry," he said. "This must be the worst first day ever for you."

"No, I've had some doozies." Her lips curved up and, though her eyes twinkled, concern radiated from them. "Do you think your sister is all right? Should I check on her?"

"I'll do it. Be right back." Still holding Grace, he retreated down the hall to speak with Belle. Grace blinked up at him, and he kissed her little nose. Then he knocked on Belle's door.

"Go away."

"I'm coming in."

"I wish you wouldn't."

"Too bad."

He slipped into her room. The closed curtains, unmade bed and darkness made the air feel thick, stale. She sat slumped on the edge of the bed with her face in her hands. He lowered his body to sit next to her, keeping a firm grip on Grace as he did.

"What's going on, sis?"

"Nothing. I'm tired."

"I know you are. It's not easy being a mama." He patted her knee. "Are you okay with Ainsley staying?"

She shrugged. "I don't know. I wish I felt good enough to take care of all the babies myself."

"Well, four is a lot. You're being too hard on yourself. I don't think most people could do it all on their own. But eventually you will, and in the meantime, I'll pop in and out to help Ainsley—until you're up to it yourself, okay?"

"Thanks, Marshall." She looked ready to cry again. "I guess I could use help with the babies."

"Good. Why don't you take a nap? I'll show Ainsley her cabin later."

"Cabin?" Her spine went rigid. "She needs to sleep here. In the main house. How else will she take care of the babies at night?"

He squeezed his eyes shut. Did his sister think Ainsley was going to work round the clock? "I hired her to help during the day."

"But you're here during the day."

All the sympathy he'd mustered disappeared. He tightened his hold on Grace.

"Belle, I can't do this. Not by myself. Not all the time."

"Well, I can't either. Do you know how hard it is to feed four babies at night?"

"Yes, I do, because you text me to come help every single night. I'm exhausted."

She dismissed his words with a backward wave. "Well, it's worse for me. You don't know. I'll have Raleigh put the blow-up mattress in the babies' room for her."

He gaped at her. "Do you hear yourself? She's not sleeping on the floor in the babies' room. She needs her own space."

Belle glared at him.

"Look, Ainsley already agreed to work ten-hour days, which is more than most people would. She'll be here from eight in the morning until six at night. You two can get the babies figured out, and when she leaves after the holidays, you'll be an old pro at it."

"But January is so soon." She looked nauseous. "You need to hire someone else. Someone permanent."

"I tried. No one replied to my ad."

After a few minutes of silence, she gave him a sheepish grin. "You couldn't have found an ugly baby nurse, could you?"

An unattractive helper would make things easier on him, but he wasn't concerned about romance. He didn't think he was capable of having a loving, committed relationship. He hadn't found a woman who understood his devotion to his sister, and he doubted he would. The only family he had was Belle and the quadruplets, and he wouldn't do anything to jeopardize it.

He patted her shoulder. "You have nothing to worry about. You're the most beautiful woman around."

"Yeah, right." She held out the bottom of her faded blue T-shirt. "You're such a liar."

"Me? Nah. I'm going back out there and making sure you didn't scare her off. Now give Grace a kiss, and we'll let you rest."

Fear flashed in her eyes so quickly he wondered if he'd imagined it. She kissed Grace's forehead and squeezed Marshall's hand. "Thanks."

He stood, hitching his chin to her. "I'll always be here for you."

With watery eyes, she nodded.

One hurdle cleared. He walked by the babies' room and heard Ben and Max stirring. Continuing into the living room, he stopped in his tracks.

Lila was strapped in her bouncy seat.

And Ainsley was gone.

Chapter Two

The babies and Marshall needed her.

Ainsley reached into the trunk of her car in search of a bag she'd packed. Snow had begun to fall, and the wind was gentler than when she'd arrived. Shivering, she stomped her feet. Her favorite blanket was folded neatly on top of her supplies, and she spotted a patch of blue beneath it—the tote with markers, stickers and charts.

Belle needed her, too, but didn't want to admit it. Ainsley kind of understood. She didn't particularly enjoy asking for help either. As long as Belle didn't resent her presence, everything would be fine.

Well, that wasn't quite true. The resentment issue wasn't the only problem. Belle didn't expect Ainsley to take over all of the babies' care, did she?

And what about Marshall? Working with

a hot, doting cowboy had better not blur her focus. She had big goals and couldn't lose sight of them. She had to take care of herself. No one else was going to.

After pulling out the tote bag, she slammed the trunk shut. She had over six weeks to make a difference in the quadruplets' lives, and she was ready to start now. She was getting these infants on a schedule.

Tightening her winter jacket around her throat, she ducked her head against the snow and scurried to the porch. The ranch house was a long, one-story wooden building with a covered porch devoid of decoration at the moment. She could imagine the posts strung with white Christmas lights and a large evergreen wreath hanging on the door.

Glancing up, she almost jumped. Marshall had stepped outside onto the faded welcome mat. He opened the door for her. "For a minute I thought you'd taken off."

She shook her hair free of snow and pushed past him into the house. "Why would you think that?"

"Well..." He scratched the back of his neck, closing the door behind them. "My sister wasn't exactly welcoming."

She took off her coat and hung it on a hook

in the entry. "Oh, no worries. She wants me to stay."

He searched her face until heat blasted her neck. Why was he looking at her so intently? With the tote over her shoulder, she strode into the living room, where both girls were in their bouncy seats, happily sucking on pacifiers. The boys' squawks from their room hadn't gone into full-blown crying…yet.

"Let's get the boys changed." She waved for him to follow her. "Then we'll figure out a way forward with these babies."

"Has anyone told you you're efficient?" He was at her side in lightning speed.

She almost laughed, continuing to the boys' crib. "Yes, and it's usually not a compliment."

"Trust me, it's a compliment. At least from me."

Ainsley picked up Ben, and Marshall took Max. Side by side they changed diapers, then went back to the living room. After settling the boys in their bouncy seats facing the girls, Ainsley and Marshall took opposite couches.

"If you're too tired to do this right now…"

"No, I'm fine." She was tired, but she wanted to get a plan nailed down as soon as possible. She placed a pouch with markers, a folder full of stickers, her trusty clipboard and the stacks of various charts she'd printed on the coffee table.

Laying them out in precise order, she reviewed the spread to make sure she wasn't missing anything. With a satisfied nod, she straightened and gave Marshall her full attention. "First, let's assign each baby a color."

"Okay." Skepticism thinned his lips.

"What?" She excelled at three things: organizing, helping those in need and reading people. "Something's bothering you."

"It's not bothering me, but...could you explain the color dealie? My expertise is not in babies. I'm good at fixing large farm equipment and taking care of cattle. I'm pretty new at quadruplets."

"Of course." She peeked at the children—all quiet, thankfully. "Each child is assigned a color, and everything will be marked with it."

"You mean their clothes?"

"Yes, we'll dot the tags with permanent marker."

"Most of their clothes don't have tags."

"Well, we'll figure it out. The clothes aren't the main thing. We'll color the bottom of each bottle. And we'll place stickers on the bouncy seats, car carriers and so on."

"Oh, I get it." He brought his hands behind his head, leaning back. She couldn't help noticing his muscular arms. "What about pacifiers and stuff?"

"I think it will be too difficult to separate pacifiers. I guess we could put them into plastic storage bins labeled with their color. We can keep marking the pinkies of Grace and Max with markers, and I think this will be another way for us to keep the twins straight. Especially at bath time when the marker might wash off."

"Good idea."

"Let's assign the colors." She slid out a sheet of red, blue, green and yellow stickers. "Who gets what?"

"I don't know." He tapped his fingertips against his jeans.

"Who's the happiest?" It would be fun to match the babies with colors representing their personalities. She waited for Marshall to reply.

"Easy. Lila."

"She gets yellow. It's the color of sunshine and joy." Ainsley held up a yellow sticker. She then placed it on a piece of paper and wrote *Lila* next to it. "Who's the most energetic?"

"Ben. Definitely. His cries go from zero to ten like that." He snapped his fingers.

"Ben gets red. The color of fire and passion." She placed the red sticker on the paper and wrote *Ben* next to it. "What about Grace and Max? Do either show signs of being a peacemaker? Or like they are attentive to the other babies' feelings? I know this might seem silly considering how young they are."

He considered it for a moment. "You know, I

think Grace does. I never realized it, but if Max and Ben are crying, she usually joins in."

"It bothers her to see her brothers upset."

"It's possible."

"She gets green, the color of nature and harmony. Does Max seem to be more stable than the other babies? Trusting?"

"He's five weeks old. I really couldn't say."

"You're right." She laughed. "Whether it suits him or not, Max gets blue, the color of the sky and stability." After writing his name, she took out another sheet of stickers, crossed to Marshall and handed him one. "Let's mark the bouncy seats, then make up bottles for the rest of the night."

"Yes, ma'am." He grinned, rising. "You're not going to ask me to put these on their foreheads, are you?"

"No, of course not." She shook her head. Marshall had a good sense of humor. Another trait she admired. She circled the bouncy seats, not seeing a good place to put the stickers. "Where do you think these should go?"

"Why don't we put a couple on each? One on the back, and we'll wrap two around the front legs."

They marked the seats and surveyed their work. It was a start. Max's pacifier fell out, and he made loud grunting noises.

"I know what that means." Marshall rolled his eyes. "I'll take this one."

She knelt in front of the other three while he changed Max. They were so little. Smaller than the average baby the same age. They looked like newborns. Humming, she placed her index finger next to Ben's fist. He flexed his hand, then curled it around her finger. The pacifier bobbed as he sucked on it.

"You're a little cutie, aren't you?" She opened her mouth and made faces at him. His hand tightened around her finger. What a sweetheart.

Marshall returned, carrying Max. "You're glad you missed that one." He waved his hand in front of his nose.

She chuckled, but it turned into a yawn. It had been a long day of packing, driving and...this.

"Hey, why don't you kick up your feet on the sofa and rest? When Belle wakes, I'll show you to your cabin."

"You don't mind? I'd like nothing more than to cuddle with these sweet babies for a while."

"Really?" He frowned as if the concept was foreign to him.

"Yes." She unstrapped Ben and took him in her arms; then she unstrapped Grace and brought both babies to the couch. "Infants grow up so fast. I'd like to enjoy this while I can."

He blinked, then followed her lead, taking Lila and Max to the other couch.

Neither spoke for several minutes. The silence gave Ainsley the space she needed to register things she'd missed. The decor was homey. A framed picture of Belle and her husband on their wedding day stood on the end table. The dining room table was stacked with supplies and a pile of what appeared to be unopened mail. In the corner, a laundry basket held stuffed animals and baby toys. Burp cloths and rattles were scattered around it. Two used bottles had rolled under the coffee table.

This was a warm home, but, from the looks of it, the babies' arrival had chilled it a bit. She'd tidy everything later. For now, she'd enjoy the wonder of two precious little ones in her arms.

Babies. How she'd love to have some of her own.

The jagged scar down her heart throbbed. Love and marriage came before kids. She didn't know if she had it in her to try that combination—even for children. Love clouded a woman's judgment. And marriage came with commitment. She couldn't cut and run from a husband the way she had from her father.

She'd stick to getting into nursing school. A career could never let her down the way love could.

* * *

"What's so funny?" Belle sounded irritated.

Marshall peered at his sister over the open refrigerator door later. Her mussed hair and puffy eyes told him she'd woken from a long nap. He hadn't seen her for hours, not since he'd talked to her about Ainsley staying. Speaking of Ainsley, she was holding one of the girls and had propped bottles up for the other three in their bouncy seats. Not one of them made a peep. Usually they took turns crying all afternoon. But the on-and-off crying session had lasted only forty-five minutes today—all because of Ainsley.

Maybe with more peace and quiet, Belle would get more involved with them. And maybe the strain between her and Raleigh would go away.

Marshall stepped back. "Oh, Ben's tongue curled over his lip when he woke up. He looked silly." He motioned for Belle. "Check this out. All the bottles you'll need for the night."

"I'll need?" She popped a hand on her hip and glowered at him. "What's that supposed to mean?"

His good mood collapsed. "Let me rephrase that. You and Raleigh will need."

"Like Raleigh will do anything." She pushed her hair behind her ear.

"Did I hear my name?" Raleigh came in through the back breezeway, his cheeks red from the cold and his hair flattened against his head from the hat he'd taken off. He shivered and rubbed his palms together. "Wait. Something's different." He squinted. "Why aren't the babies crying?"

Belle studied her fingernails.

Marshall waved for Raleigh to join him in the living room. "Come and meet Ainsley Draper."

"Oh, right, the baby nurse."

Ainsley winced as she hauled herself to her feet. Guilt tugged on Marshall's conscience. She'd been helping with the babies since the minute she'd arrived, and she looked worn out. After Raleigh grinned and wiggled his fingers at the babies, Marshall made the introductions.

"I sure am glad to have you here, Ainsley." Raleigh jerked his thumb toward Marshall. "It's been brutal not having him helping me with the cattle."

She smiled politely. Marshall didn't know what to say. These were Raleigh's babies, for crying out loud. Didn't the man care that the quadruplets needed him more than the cows did? He had other ranch hands. It wasn't as if Marshall was indispensable out there.

"Seeing how the ladies have the babies under control, you'll be out tomorrow to prep for the cattle sale, right?" The tall, lean man with piercing blue eyes had *tough* written all over him. Raleigh had grown up on this ranch working the land with his father.

"No, Raleigh, he won't." Belle charged into the room. "Marshall promised he'd be around to help Ainsley."

"Why can't you?" he asked quietly, a defiant glint in his eyes.

"I can't believe you even asked that."

Marshall could feel the tension building. Grace's bottle rolled out of her mouth and she began to cry.

"See what you did?" Belle pointed to the baby, then to Raleigh. "She was fine until you marched in here. You're so loud."

"Come on," Marshall said to Ainsley. He knew where this was heading, and he didn't want Ainsley getting any more reasons to leave. "It's been a long day. I'll show you to your cabin."

She nodded, setting Lila in her seat before going to the hall to get her coat and bag.

He glanced over his shoulder. "Belle, there's a casserole from one of the church ladies in the oven. Give it thirty minutes. We'll see you tomorrow."

"You're leaving?"

He didn't respond. Instead, he swiped his coat and cowboy hat before ushering Ainsley outside. He led the way to her car. After opening the door for her and waiting for her to get in, he leaned over. "Follow the drive around the house and stay left. You'll see a row of cabins. Park in front of the first one. I'll unlock it for you."

"Don't you want a ride?"

"Nah, I like the fresh air. Clears my head." He straightened and shut her door.

Once her engine started, he hiked down the driveway to the cabins. Darkness had fallen, and the wind drove small snow pellets to the ground. He shrugged into his jacket collar and shoved his hands into his pockets.

What was going on between Belle and Raleigh? Part of him wanted to rush back to the house and make sure she was okay. But Raleigh had never gotten physical with her, unlike their mother's boyfriends. Still, Marshall didn't like the dynamic he'd been seeing lately. Raleigh seemed to resent Belle, and Belle sassed him on a regular basis. Not that Marshall blamed her…

He sighed. He'd keep trying to do his best to make life easier on them. He'd quit a job he'd enjoyed to help out with the quads, and it wasn't like Belle had planned on having four babies at once. Who could have predicted the two embryos implanted would split into two sets of identical twins?

Belle needed him.

And he'd be there for her. Even if he didn't like the ranch life very much and wasn't good at baby care.

Ainsley's car passed him, and he pushed his legs to move faster. When he reached her cabin, she was standing behind the open trunk. He unlocked the front door of her cabin and adjusted the thermostat higher. He'd stopped in last night to give it a quick cleaning. The one-bedroom log structure should meet her needs.

The stomping of feet made him pivot. Snow outlined her shoes on the mat inside the front door. She passed through the short hallway lined with a bench and hooks for coats and scarves.

"This is cute." She craned her neck side to side to take the space in.

The gleaming log walls gave it a cozy feel. Lighter hardwood floors matched the wooden beams of the ceiling. The right half of the room consisted of a square wooden table with two chairs next to the rustic kitchenette. The left half was a living area with a tan-and-white-checked couch, recliner, coffee table and a television on a stand. Windows hid behind tan curtains on each wall, and area rugs protected feet from the chill.

"Here, let me get your bags." He took the suitcases from her grasp, his fingers brushing hers in the process. A surge of warmth raced up his arms. "Follow me. I'll give you the tour. Dining. Living. Kitchen. Sorry, no dishwasher, but everything else works fine. Anything not on the open shelves, you'll find in the cupboards." He strode through the small space to the back. "Bathroom to the right. Bedroom to the left."

"Oh, I wasn't expecting this." She set her purse on the bed. With her finger trailing the puffy white duvet, she rounded the footboard and pushed open the curtains of one of the windows in the snug bedroom. "It's lovely."

He lined her suitcases against the wall and stepped back to survey it. He supposed she was right. The white curtains had a tan curlicue design. Fluffy white rugs were on the floor—nothing a cowboy would buy for sure.

"I'm guessing I have a view of the mountains during the daytime." She let the curtain fall across the window again.

"You sure do. I have the same view. I'm right next door."

Her long lashes curled to her eyebrows, and those green-gold eyes arrested him, made him lose his train of thought. Now that he was putting two and two together, this cabin was feminine like her. His had the same layout, but his beams and floor were dark like the walls, and the furniture was masculine. In the months he'd lived on Dushane Ranch, no one had ever stayed in this cabin. Until now.

She looked like she belonged here.

His female interaction had been limited to Belle for longer than he cared to admit. And now was not a good time for that to change.

He hooked his thumbs in his belt loops. "I'll let you get settled. Come next door in, say, thirty minutes. I'll have supper waiting for you." He spun on his heel to leave.

"You don't have to make me supper."

He strode to the entrance, wishing her words were true. Would make life easier if he wasn't around someone so pretty and nice, but he would be, and he couldn't let her starve.

"It's no trouble. There are only a few dried goods in here." He tipped his hat to her. "See you in half an hour."

Out on the porch, the clean, frigid air froze his nostrils, and he almost laughed. Winter in Wyoming. Good thing he didn't mind cold weather. Too bad he didn't like the situation he was in. Cowboying for his tough-as-nails brother-in-law. Soothing his poor sister. Caring for his nephews and nieces. And fighting an unanticipated attraction to the baby nurse.

He must be out of his mind to stay.

What was the alternative? He'd rather be here with Belle and his nieces and nephews than out there with no one.

Being out of his mind beat being lonely any day of the week.

What a bizarre day.

Ainsley finished stacking her sweaters, leggings and jeans in the dresser, then went to the living room and sprawled out on the couch. She still had fifteen minutes before heading next door. After hours of baby care and trying to make sense of Belle's baffling behavior, Ainsley wasn't sure what to think of being the baby nurse on Dushane Ranch. Was Belle really just tired, or was she neglecting her children? Maybe Marshall could give her some insight about his sister tonight.

It would give her something to think about other than the fact she would be eating with the hunky cowboy who impressed her with his devotion. Frankly, he seemed a little too good to be true.

The man must have a flaw.

They all did.

She took in the room. A soothing retreat. Unfussy. The furniture was neutral, the wooden walls and floors inviting. Even the open shelves in the kitchen pleased the eye with their collection of white dishes. She'd enjoy coming home to this every day.

She had a feeling she was going to need a restful place to decompress each night. The babies were not a problem as far as she was concerned. Their parents on the other hand...

Belle and Raleigh were already stressing her out, and she'd been here less than twenty-four hours. She'd never been around a mother who wasn't hovering over her infant. Sure, quadruplets were vastly different from one child, but shouldn't Belle have shown a sliver of interest in holding and feeding them? She'd practically thrown Lila into Ainsley's arms earlier before vanishing.

Then there was Raleigh. Typical rancher. The man probably paid more attention to the calves in the pastures than his own babies. Ainsley was used to men like him. Her father had been cut from the same cloth. He'd worked on several ranches when she was little.

Thinking about her dad always pinched her heart. He loved her in his own way. She loved him, too. But she hadn't been able to stick around and watch him destroy his life. His love for her had never matched his love of alcohol.

Leaving him had been like stabbing a knife in her own heart. It still hurt. Probably always would.

She glanced at her watch. The fifteen minutes were up. She shoved her feet into boots, eased into her coat, then strolled next door. A path through the snow had been cleared between the cabins. About twenty feet separated their porch steps. Her spirits lightened as she watched her breath materialize in wispy puffs. One of the wonders of winter.

His porch light was on, and a shovel with snow caked on the bottom was propped against the side rail. The man was thoughtful. Another thing to add to his growing list of virtues.

She knocked on the door and heard, "coming," and then Marshall stood before her with a ladle in hand. He grinned. "You didn't get lost."

"It wasn't hard to find." She gave him a smile, taking off her coat and boots. She blew on her hands. "What can I help with?"

"You can set the table." He backtracked to the kitchenette, identical to hers, except everything in this cabin was dark wood. The place reeked of masculinity. While it suited him, she preferred her pretty space.

Plates, bowls, silverware and paper napkins had been piled near the edge of the table. She made up two place settings. The unmistakable aroma of chili filled the air. He tossed her a pot holder, and she caught it, setting it on the table.

"Hope you're not a vegetarian," he said.

"Isn't that illegal in Wyoming?"

His laugh was low and hearty. It sent flutters through her chest. After carrying the chili to the table, he hustled back to the oven and pulled out a cast-iron pan of corn bread.

"Wow, when did you have time to do all this?" She took a seat at the table.

"I didn't have to. The slow cooker did all the work." He ladled chili into each of their bowls. She cut the corn bread into slices and set one on his plate.

His spoon was poised above his food, but she cleared her throat. He glanced up.

"Would you like me to say grace?" she asked.

He set the spoon down and folded his hands.

"Dear Lord, thank You for this delicious meal. Please let it nourish us and give us the strength to care for Your precious babies tomorrow. In Jesus's name, amen."

"Amen."

"Marshall?" She slathered butter on her corn bread. "Would you mind telling me more about Belle and Raleigh?"

His eyebrows drew together, and he seemed really into his food. "What do you want to know?"

"How long have they been married? How did they end up with quadruplets?" *Why is your sister ambivalent about the babies?* She took a bite of chili. Spicy, meaty, it hit the spot. "By the way, this is absolutely delicious."

"Thanks." The side of his mouth tweaked upward. "They've been married for three years.

Raleigh had cancer in his early twenties and the doctors advised him the treatment would affect his chances at having children, so he took the advice of a fertility specialist. Belle was well aware the only way they'd have biological children was with medical help. They started the process right after the honeymoon. Their first attempts didn't take. They decided to try in vitro fertilization. Two embryos were implanted. They both split. And two sets of identical twins were born."

"That must have been shocking. I had no idea." She ran through a few mental calculations. Belle would have been on hormone therapy before getting pregnant. Then the fact she was having four babies would have sent her natural hormones into overdrive. Since she'd given birth five weeks ago, there was a good chance her entire body was out of whack. "So I take it both of them wanted the babies?"

"Oh, yeah. They were ecstatic when they heard the news. Honestly, up until she gave birth, Belle was happier than I'd ever seen her."

"And Raleigh?"

"I don't know." He turned his attention to the chili. "He's hard to read."

His attitude confused her. He positively lit up talking about Belle, but when the topic changed to Raleigh, he shut down. She thought about her first impression of Raleigh. He'd beamed at the babies before he'd spoken to her. Sure, he'd been more concerned with having Marshall back on ranch duties than with what the babies needed, but did it make him a bad parent?

"I'm hoping with you here—" Marshall glanced at her "—some of the pressure will be off Belle."

"Pressure? You mean with the babies?" She hadn't been deaf to the undercurrents in the conversation back at the main house. Belle wanted help with the quads. Raleigh wanted help with the ranch. And Marshall wanted…what did he want?

"Yeah." He took another bite, and she took the opportunity to study his face. His handsome features and strong bone structure weren't enough to hide the fact he looked completely exhausted, as if he hadn't had a full night's rest in a week.

What if he hadn't? He'd mentioned stopping over in the wee hours to help Belle sometimes, but surely he hadn't meant every night?

No. She almost shook her head. Belle and Raleigh were there. Between the two of them, they could manage feeding the quadruplets.

Lost in her thoughts, she continued to enjoy the meal. The lamp next to the couch cast a welcoming glow on the living room, and the overhead lights added a cozy cheerfulness to the small room. The light whoosh of the wind outside added to the atmosphere. A pleasant place to enjoy a hot meal on a night like this.

"What about you, Ainsley?" He met her eyes, and she felt exposed, like he could see right into her heart. "You made it clear you'd only be here through the holidays. What do you have lined up after that?"

"I applied for a job at the hospital in Laramie. I'm trying to get into the nursing program at the university. I already have my first two years out of the way, but the program is competitive. I didn't make the cut last year."

He pushed his empty bowl back. "So this job at the hospital is in nursing?"

"No, I'd be a monitor technician in the ICU. It's great experience." She couldn't wait to hear back from the hospital. They'd be making their decision in a few weeks. With her letters of recommendation, she had a very good chance at the job. And it would be one more plus on her application to nursing school.

"I'm impressed. I'm not much into blood and guts. Well, unless you count the guts of a tractor."

She polished off the final bite of her chili. His eyes were brighter. He didn't look as tired. "You can fix a tractor?"

"Yes, ma'am. I used to work in Cheyenne for a large equipment repair shop. Loved it."

"What happened?"

He shrugged. "When Belle found out about the babies, well, she and I are twins and we're all we've got. No mom, no dad. Just us. I wasn't going to leave her here to do it on her own."

"But she's not on her own. She has Raleigh, right?"

He straightened, adjusting his shirt. "I don't expect you to understand."

Quietly, she picked up her plate and bowl and took them to the sink. She understood as much as she needed to. Either Raleigh wasn't a great husband or Marshall didn't think his sister could handle much.

Something was off about his relationship with Belle. She could sense it.

Maybe he did have a flaw, after all.

Chapter Three

❧

"We aren't paying you to leave the babies unattended."

Ainsley wiped her damp hands on the hand towel and counted to five. Belle had finally opted to emerge from her room, and, as Ainsley had found out repeatedly over the past week, she'd come prepared to criticize. The eight-to-six schedule had been a nice fantasy. So had getting a day off. Every morning Ainsley arrived at seven thirty and couldn't in good conscience leave until after seven, when Marshall and Raleigh returned from their evening chores. Though Marshall helped with the babies for a few hours each morning and in the afternoon, the bulk of the care fell to her. She wouldn't mind, but Belle rarely touched the infants, and being treated like the hired help was getting old.

"I had to use the bathroom." She walked by

Belle, who stood with one hip jutted out and a sour expression on her face. Ben started fussing. She mustered the last scraps of her patience. "The babies are about ready to eat. Why don't you sit on the couch, and I'll hand the boys to you?"

"Why the boys? Why not the girls?" Belle backed up a step, alarm running a fifty-meter dash in her eyes. Ainsley was too tired to feel sympathetic. Max let out a whimper, and Ben's fussing turned into crying. She'd tried to engage Belle many times since arriving last week, but she'd yet to see Belle holding a baby. Ainsley kept trying, though.

"Fine. I'll bring the girls to you. Let me warm their bottles. I'll be right back." She trudged to the kitchen and took out four bottles from the refrigerator. The sound of Grace joining the crying made her lean her elbows on the counter and drop her head. She'd learned the hard way that crying was contagious. The longer it went on, the harder it was to contain. It took everything inside her not to yell to Belle to pick up one of the babies and try to comfort them.

The woman had zero baby skills.

Or maybe she had no confidence.

Either way, Ainsley wanted to take her by the shoulders and shake her. *Don't you want to be their mother? What is wrong with you?*

From the living room, she heard Lila's little cry. *Lord, this is bad if even sweet Lila is crying. Why am I here? I can't make a difference if their mother refuses to hold them. What will happen after the holidays when I leave?*

As she warmed the bottles, tension gripped her throat. The babies' cries grew more insistent. She tested two of the bottles—lukewarm—and marched back to the living room, ready to force Belle to feed a set of twins if need be.

But one look at the woman and she halted. Belle stood over the bouncy seats with her hands down by her sides. A trail of tears rushed down her cheeks, and her fingers were trembling.

How had Ainsley missed it?

Belle wasn't an ambivalent mother. And this wasn't a lack of confidence—this was naked fear.

Could Belle have postpartum depression?

The truth pierced her to the core. Ainsley needed to approach her differently. She pulled her shoulders back and calmly approached Belle. Using her most soothing voice, she said, "Go ahead and sit on the couch. Lila wants her mommy."

Belle hastily wiped her tears away. "I… I'm really tired." She took a step toward the hall, but Ainsley blocked her way.

"I know you're tired. Sit with Lila. She's so

cuddly. You can rest on the couch, and I'll put the television on."

Belle licked her cracked lips. "I don't know—"

Ainsley put her arm around her, steered her to the couch and handed her a bottle. Then she unstrapped Lila, cooed some baby talk to her and placed her in Belle's arms. Belle stiffened, but Ainsley pretended not to notice.

"See? She's better already." Ainsley said a silent prayer of thanks when Lila stopped crying. She held her breath, waiting to see if Belle would offer the bottle to the baby. She did. And visibly relaxed. "I'll get the boys' bottles and be right back."

Thank You, Lord!

Ainsley rolled up receiving blankets and propped the boys' bottles on them in their bouncy seats. They both calmed immediately. Then she picked up Grace and sat on the other couch to feed her. With the babies quiet again, Ainsley turned on the television.

"What do you like to watch?"

"I don't care." Belle actually smiled at Lila.

"Well, with Thanksgiving a few days away, let's drool over the cooking shows." She clicked to the food channel and relaxed into the couch. Grace was warm and happy, and for the first time in days, Ainsley had a sense of peace.

Postpartum depression she could deal with.

The color-coding and schedule had helped tremendously, too, but things had to change around here. If they didn't, Belle wouldn't be able to care for the babies on her own. And Ainsley couldn't work twelve-hour days seven days a week or she'd get burned out.

Marshall came to mind. She hadn't asked him about it, but she suspected he stopped by regularly to help with the babies at night. They weren't doing Belle, Raleigh or the children any favors by doing all the work. Grace finished her bottle, so Ainsley lifted her to burp her. Darling little thing. Funny how the exhaustion and frustration dissipated as soon as one of the babies was in her arms.

"What do you and Raleigh usually do for Thanksgiving?" Ainsley patted Grace's back and glanced at Belle.

She got a faraway look in her eyes, making her appear softer. "Since neither of us has any family left, I like to make a big dinner." Her face fell. "But I don't know about this year. It's all too much."

"If we help with the babies, would you want to make the dinner?" Maybe doing something she enjoyed would get Belle in a better frame of mind.

"I... I don't know. It's a lot of work." Worry lines creased her forehead.

"Yes, it is." Ainsley didn't want her over-whelmed. "Maybe one of the guys could help you with cooking. I'm not very good in the kitchen."

Belle turned to face her. She seemed to perk up. "No? Well, Raleigh is hopeless unless he's grilling. I'll ask Marshall."

The fact Belle automatically fell back on Marshall concerned her. It was as if he was at her beck and call.

And he never turned his sister down.

Uneasiness slithered down her spine.

Ainsley could write the book on codependent relationships. She'd been in one with her father for twenty-one years. Three years ago, she'd broken free, and she'd promised herself she'd never be in one again.

Whatever was going on with Marshall and his sister didn't seem healthy. If he didn't set some boundaries, Ainsley didn't know if she could stick out this baby nurse stint to completion. She'd discuss it with him at dinner. She just hoped he'd listen—for his sake, for Belle's and, most of all, for the babies'.

Life was finally starting to feel manageable. Marshall finished brushing his horse and led him to the stall. After feeding and watering the animal, he strode back to his cabin. High winds had left the ground dry. It was almost 7:00 p.m., and his porch light beckoned under the dark sky. Inside his cabin, he took off his winter outerwear before scrubbing his hands and checking his appearance in the bathroom mirror.

Bags hung low beneath bloodshot eyes. His scruff had grown to an unruly level. He looked terrible.

What did he expect? He hadn't gotten more than four hours of sleep at a time since the babies had come home from the hospital. He didn't want to tell Ainsley, but Belle called him every night at around 1:00 a.m. in a panic. And worry twisted his insides until he figured it was best to run over and get the babies settled. It didn't take long. They'd need a change and a bottle and they'd drift back to sleep in no time.

But then he'd get a text at 5:00 a.m., as well. And since Raleigh was out feeding cattle before that, Marshall knew she was all alone. So, he'd stop in at the main house. Running back and forth between the ranch and the babies left him exhausted.

After making himself presentable, he went to the kitchen and turned on the oven. He'd thawed out barbecue pulled pork earlier. He tossed it into a baking dish and slid it along with some frozen French fries into the oven. Then he threw on his coat and went out the door. If he didn't collect Ainsley from the main house, she'd be there all night.

Guilt slowed his pace on the path. Ainsley was working twelve-hour days. He wanted to believe Belle was doing her fair share of the baby care, but deep down, he knew she wasn't. And since he'd been Raleigh's right-hand man for the calf sale, he'd been unable to help as much. Thankfully, as of yesterday, all the calves had shipped, and the ranch was back to normal operations.

As he'd ridden around the pastures all afternoon, he'd had one thing on his mind—and it wasn't calves.

Dinner with Ainsley. His favorite part of the day.

After a quick knock on the back door, he let himself in. None of the babies was crying, which was a relief. He stopped when the living room came in view. Belle sat on one of the couches, and she cradled Lila in her arms. Ainsley was on her knees in front of the bouncy seats, holding a stuffed puppy up to Ben. She rose, turned and spotted Marshall. She brought her finger to her lips, nudging her head at Belle.

He placed his hand over his heart. His sister actually looked like she was enjoying holding the baby. His relief was so sweet it almost brought tears.

Things were finally turning around.

The sound of Raleigh stomping his boots in the breezeway made Marshall's gut clench. *Please, don't say something stupid, Raleigh.*

He entered the room, the tang of winter air on his clothes, and he stopped short. Marshall wanted to say something, to warn him not to ruin it, but to his surprise, Raleigh padded over to Belle and put his hand on her shoulder. "She sure likes her mama, doesn't she?"

Belle covered his hand with hers, then quickly slipped it back under Lila.

Ainsley crossed the room to Marshall.

"Let's give them some privacy," she whispered.

They strode together to his cabin, neither speaking. He had so much he wanted to say, to ask, but a part of him wondered if it was better not to know. Whatever he'd just witnessed was a blessing, and he'd accept it.

He opened the door for her, and the aroma of barbecue made his stomach growl.

"I can't tell you how incredible this smells." Ainsley hung up her coat and crossed to his shelves, taking down two plates as she'd done every night since arriving.

He enjoyed their routine. While she set the table, he found hot pads and took the food out of the oven.

"Thank you so much for feeding me," she

said. "I feel bad you're doing all the cooking, but I can barely make instant oatmeal. Frozen foods are my best friends."

"It's the least I can do." He set the pulled pork on the table and went back for the fries. "I know this hasn't been easy on you. Whatever you did back there to get Belle holding the baby, well… I can't thank you enough."

He waited until Ainsley finished saying the prayer before serving up the food.

She picked up a fry. "I think your sister has postpartum depression."

His fork clattered to the table. *Postpartum depression?*

"She needs to see a doctor." Ainsley took a bite.

"But she was better today. She was holding Lila. She looked happy." The words came out too fast. He didn't know what to think.

"I know. Today was a good start. But I'm not going to be here long. And she needs to be able to handle all four babies."

"One will lead to another. And I'll stop by as much as I can."

Ainsley wiped her mouth with her napkin and looked him in the eye.

"That's another thing we need to talk about. I know you think you're helping by going over there at night—"

"I *think* I'm helping? As far as I can tell, I *am* helping." He pushed his chair back, rubbing his hand over his stubble.

"You're right, you are helping. But neither of us can sustain this. And we shouldn't. From my perspective, you and I act more like parents to these babies than either Belle or Raleigh. We cover the brunt of their care."

He tilted his chin up. "That's why I hired you." As soon as he said it, he regretted it.

Her eyes softened. "You didn't hire me to be their mother."

"I know." He slumped, his appetite gone. "I didn't mean it like that."

She covered his hand with hers, and he was surprised at how comforting her touch felt. "Marshall, you need sleep. And we both need a day off. Your sister and brother-in-law are taking advantage of you. And I didn't agree to work seven days a week, twelve hours a day. I'm getting burned out, and I think you are, too."

He couldn't argue. He knew it was true. But what was the alternative?

"I want to stay, but…" She averted her eyes.

Wait? She *wanted* to stay? Was she considering leaving? His heartbeat galloped as the few bites of dinner he'd eaten threatened to come up.

She continued. "If I'm going to stay, we both have to work together for the quadruplets' best interests."

If she was going to stay? He shook his head to clear the panic. He didn't succeed. "What are you suggesting?"

"We stick to set hours. From now on, I'm arriving at eight and leaving at six whether your sister likes it or not. And you have to stop going over there in the night. If she can't handle it, Raleigh needs to step up. He's their father."

He swallowed. He knew she spoke the truth. Raleigh should be on night duty with Belle. Still, Marshall didn't know if he could go through with what Ainsley was asking.

"We both are taking Sundays off." She took a dainty bite of pork.

Sundays off? She was backing him into a corner.

"I don't see how I can." He massaged the back of his neck. "She hasn't been alone with the babies for an entire day."

"Raleigh will be with her. He was in and out all day last Sunday. He can leave the ranch chores to the other hands for one day of the week."

"Neither Belle nor Raleigh knows what to do, though. What will happen to the little ones?"

She flattened her palms on either side of her plate and leaned forward. "You didn't know what to do, and you figured it out. They will, too. We'll train them. Show them the color-coding. Give them the schedule. They have to start taking care of these babies, Marshall."

A splitting headache was coming on. But she was right. He kept hoping Belle would suddenly become a capable mother, and he'd ignored the fact Raleigh should be on diaper duty, too. What did that say about him?

"And one more thing." She lowered her lashes before meeting his gaze straight on. "Belle needs to see a doctor. Postpartum depression is nothing to mess around with. I don't think she'll listen to me, but you? She'll hear you out."

Ugh. He'd officially lost his appetite.

"You're telling me I need to convince my sister to see a doctor for postpartum depression? No way."

"Then I'm sorry, but I have to turn in my notice. I'm not going to spend the next five weeks of my life being the sole caregiver to four babies while their mother hides in her room and their father is too busy with work to feed or change them. Belle needs medical help."

She couldn't quit! He stood and stalked to the kitchen counter. What was he supposed to do? How could he convince her to stay without agreeing to her demands?

What she was asking was too hard.

He'd been faced with impossible decisions before. One had left Belle vulnerable, alone. And it had been the last time he'd seen his mother.

He took a deep breath. This was different. Ainsley wasn't willfully blind like his mother— if anything, she saw too much.

He didn't like it, but what choice did he have? He couldn't let Ainsley leave. It would benefit no one.

"Fine. Sundays off. I'll talk to Belle."

"And you won't go over to help with the babies at night anymore?"

He gritted his teeth. "I won't go over at night."

She flashed a smile. "Then, I'll stay."

He should be relieved, but was he letting his sister down? She wasn't going to be happy when he refused to come over tonight. And broaching the subject of postpartum depression? He'd rather get the flu…or flesh-eating bacteria.

When was the last time he'd told his sister no?

Staring out the window, he realized he rarely refused her requests.

He was so tired. Why couldn't Belle snap out of it? And why wasn't Raleigh caring for the babies at night already? He stole a peek at Ainsley, who wore a serene expression as she ate.

Regret punched him in the gut. Had he been taking advantage of Ainsley?

And in his rush to help Belle, had he been hurting his sister?

He closed his eyes. It was time to change things, the way Ainsley said. He just prayed Belle would forgive him.

Chapter Four

If he could take a snapshot of one moment to represent everything about his sister he'd missed since she'd given birth, this would be it. Harmony. Quality time with her. Marshall poked Belle as she dumped brown sugar into the bowl of yams. She gave him the death glare, but a smile teased her lips. In the background, television announcers introduced another float in the parade, and Ainsley's and Raleigh's voices could just be made out from the living room.

"What next?" With a knife, Marshall scraped the chopped potatoes into a large pan.

"You can cut up the herbs for the dressing while I finish these yams." Belle sprinkled some ginger and cinnamon into the bowl. "Thanks for helping, Marsh."

"I can't think of anything I'd rather be doing, Belle." He peered around the corner to check on

Ainsley. Well, that was stretching the truth. He liked feeding the babies with Ainsley. She'd set one of the girls on a blanket on the floor. Raleigh stood over them, his face perplexed as he rubbed his chin. She took a fresh diaper and laid it next to the baby. Then she pointed for him to hand her a wipe. After cleaning up the child, she put the new diaper on, snapped the coverall shut and cradled her to her chest. He heard her say, "Now you try it."

"Are you going to stand there all day?" Belle had her sassy tone on. "Come on. Chop. Chop."

He tore his gaze away from Raleigh, who was kneeling down, flipping the diaper and peering at the sticky tabs with a dumbfounded expression.

"Did you know your husband is changing a diaper at this very moment?" He rinsed the herbs, setting them on a paper towel to dry.

"I don't believe you." Belle's eyes grew round. He nodded. She stuck her head around the cupboard, then jerked it back. "Well, I never thought I'd see the day."

"Why not?" Marshall tried to keep his tone light. The fact Raleigh hadn't been changing diapers irritated him. Didn't the man care they were all chipping in to help with his children?

"You know Raleigh." She sniffed. After a few

stirs, she poured the yam mixture into a baking dish.

"Not really." Marshall didn't pretend to know much about the man she'd married. Raleigh was a strong guy, cared about the ranch and cattle and his employees. He didn't talk much. And he didn't seem to support Belle the way she needed.

"Well, he's not like Ed."

Marshall clenched his jaw. The knife slipped from his hand, clattering into the sink. Hearing Ed's name rattled him. Their mother's fourth—or was it fifth?—low-life boyfriend, Ed, had moved in when they were twelve. He'd slapped Marshall around and yelled at him for no reason. Marshall could handle getting knocked about and shouted at, but he couldn't handle the way Ed stared at Belle. He would sit too close to her. Pinch her. As the months wore on, Ed's preoccupation with Belle increased. And Marshall's disgust and fear and anger had magnified, too. He'd told their mother Ed was getting touchy-feely with Belle. And she hadn't believed him. His pleas with his mother to dump Ed had been ignored.

Marshall had tried to protect Belle. He told her to run to the apartment upstairs and stay with her friend Tiffany if he wasn't around. But the day their mother announced they were all moving into Ed's house, Marshall realized the little protection Belle had from living in the apartment would be gone. He told his mom he'd kill Ed before moving there.

"Marsh?" Belle asked. "Are you listening?"

He cleared his mind of the troubling thoughts. "Sorry, what?"

"I love Raleigh, but I wish he didn't expect me to be the world's best mom. If he helped at night…oh, forget it. No sense wishing."

"What if he *did* help with the babies at night?" Marshall leaned against the counter. "Would it take some of the pressure off you?"

"I don't know." Her voice sounded small. "I feel like I should be able to handle it on my own."

Marshall's muscles tensed. He still hadn't broached the subject of not coming over on nights or Sundays. And he certainly hadn't touched the topic of seeing a doctor. But maybe Belle was more receptive to getting help than he'd thought.

"I think you're going through a lot more than most new parents are prepared for. Don't be so hard on yourself. Want me to talk to Raleigh about helping with the babies at night?"

She glanced up through watery eyes and nodded.

"It will be better for you if he's helping instead of me." He patted the herbs dry and started cutting them. "And I'm sure you're missing your alone time with Raleigh, too. Ainsley and I are going to be taking Sundays off from now on. That way you and Raleigh and the quads can get used to each other and you'll have some space."

"What? We don't need space. We need help with the babies."

He paused, shifting to face her. "Well, Ainsley and I need a day off."

"Fine." She slammed a cupboard shut. "You and *Ainsley* take your day off. I'll never get a day off again, but who am I to complain? Pass me the pepper."

"It's not like that." He handed her the pepper shaker.

"Then what is it like? It sure seems like history repeating itself."

He stilled. "What are you talking about?"

"Don't pretend getting sent to the group home wasn't a relief. You got out. And I was stuck."

He stepped back, shaking his head slowly. "How can you say that? The group home was a prison sentence. You know it killed me to not be with you, to not be able to protect you."

Her eyes grew dark, hard. "Yeah, well, no one protected me. I ran away and learned to protect myself, but I can't run away from this." She spread her arms to take in the bottles and formula.

"Why would you want to?" He was still reel-ing from her accusations. He'd failed her—he'd lived with it for many years—but it still hurt hearing her say it.

"I don't," she said too quickly. "I love the children."

"Then why would you say it?"

"You know me." She flushed. "I say stupid stuff sometimes. Forget it. Let's leave the past behind us and enjoy today."

He closed the gap between them and hugged her. "I'm sorry I couldn't protect you. It still hurts me, Belle. More than you'll ever know."

"I needed you, Marsh." She stepped back. "Not just because of Ed… I needed my brother."

"I needed you, too. And I'll always be here for you." He resumed chopping the herbs, although with more force than before. The hum of the microwave halted with a beep.

Ainsley approached with flushed cheeks and sparkly eyes. "Can I squeeze in to warm up some bottles?"

"Of course." Marshall moved aside. She wore a green sweater and formfitting jeans. Her hair was loosely braided to the side. She looked fresh and pretty.

"Everything okay out there?" Belle asked.

"Oh, yes. Max is entertaining his daddy." Ainsley's face glowed. She sure looked happy.

"Mmm…it smells so good in here. Thanks for making dinner. I can't wait until it's ready."

"Should be an hour or so." Belle's tone set Marshall back.

Did his sister have a problem with Ainsley? Belle's reactions and emotions had been all over the place for weeks. He didn't know what to think. But at least he'd come through on one of his promises to Ainsley. They now had Sundays off. And with her showing Raleigh the basics, Raleigh could help Belle if she needed it at night.

As for talking to his sister about seeing a doctor, it wasn't necessary. Obviously, Belle was nervous about taking care of four babies. And after surviving their childhood, Marshall couldn't blame her. With some time and patience, Belle would be back to herself. And maybe someday she'd forgive him for not being around when she'd needed him the most.

"I married the finest cook in Wyoming." Raleigh beamed at Belle. "Would you pass the turkey, please?"

Ainsley glanced back and forth between Belle and Raleigh and let out a sigh of relief. Thanksgiving was going well. They seemed to be enjoying each other, unlike yesterday when Raleigh had stopped in during the afternoon. Belle had been in her room resting, and he'd gone to check on her. Within minutes, Belle had started shouting at him, and he'd stormed out, his face set, and retreated to the barn or wherever he went after one of their fights.

Ben squirmed in Ainsley's arms, and she shifted him, smiling at his adorable face. He'd been fussy all morning. With the other three babies napping, Ainsley had decided to hold him during dinner.

"Everything is delicious." She peeked at Marshall, who was buttering a roll. He met her eyes and smiled. Her cheeks grew as warm as the piping-hot food on the table.

"Thank you," Belle said. "And thanks, Marshall, for helping me. You might have overdone it on the sage, but the dressing is still mouthwatering."

Ben made a noise, screwing up his little face. He'd been unhappy most of the day, and Ainsley couldn't figure out why.

"Is he all right? Does he need a bottle?" Raleigh sounded gruff but concerned.

"He's fine. A little fussy. He might have a tummy ache." Ainsley shifted the boy to burp him. She gently patted his back and stole a bite of food when she could.

"Should I call the doctor?" Belle had paled.

Ainsley waved her concern away. "No, no. This is normal. Some babies fuss all day long.

And if they have colic, they cry nonstop. This is nothing to worry about."

"Well, when should we worry?" Belle gripped the fork in her hands, her knuckles turning white.

Why was Belle so tense? Ainsley ran her hand over Ben's fuzzy hair. "If one of the babies has a fever, isn't eating, is lethargic—basically if they seem like they aren't themselves—that's when you call a doctor."

One of the babies cried from the other room. Belle, still pale, didn't move. Raleigh covered her hand with his. "It's okay, I've got this one. You cooked all morning. Sit and enjoy the meal."

Belle's eyes grew wider than a full moon, and Ainsley almost chuckled. She met Marshall's gaze, which told her he was as surprised as she was. Moments later, Raleigh returned holding Grace like she was made of glass.

"Should I feed her?" Raleigh didn't look comfortable.

Ainsley didn't need to check the chart to know Grace had taken a bottle an hour prior with the other babies. "No, try a binkie."

Marshall stood, clapping Raleigh on the shoulder. "I'll get her a pacifier."

"Thanks." Relief chased away the concern as he smiled down at Grace. "Smelling all this food woke you up, didn't it, pretty girl? Just wait until you get to eat your mama's home cooking."

Ben had stopped fussing, so Ainsley tucked him in the crook of her arm. She continued eating the turkey and mashed potatoes on her plate. She'd steered clear of the cranberry relish. An unfortunate incident with a canned version as a child had turned her off from the jellylike dish for life.

Marshall returned and handed Raleigh the pacifier. Grace instantly settled down.

"Well, will you look at that." Raleigh sounded delightfully surprised.

They all resumed eating. The atmosphere in the house was so pleasant for once. Ainsley couldn't think of anywhere she'd rather be than right here to celebrate the holiday. For a brief moment she wondered what her father was doing now. As far as she knew, he wandered the countryside as a cowboy for hire.

If she had to guess, he was eating a frozen turkey dinner and then holing up at a local bar until closing time. Holidays had never been his strong suit. What had been, really?

He tried, Ainsley. There were times he tried. He taught you how to ride horses, made sure you took driver's training and even came to one of your high school volleyball games.

She blinked away sudden tears, wishing his life could have turned out differently and that she could still be in it.

"Ainsley, would you like another roll?" Marshall held out a basket to her.

"No, thank you." She inhaled, shaking her head politely. She knew better than to think about the past. It was better to focus on the present. Holding a baby and eating a real turkey dinner was a vast improvement from most of her Thanksgivings, including the previous two years when she'd waited tables.

When she'd been younger, she'd had fantasies about celebrating with a large extended family and playing games and watching Christmas movies all afternoon. Today was the closest she'd gotten to that fantasy.

"What do you all do after dinner?" Ainsley asked. "Do you have any traditions?"

Belle met Raleigh's gaze and a grin spread across her face. He groaned.

"We always play a game." Belle's nose scrunched in mischief.

"Can we please skip it this year?" Raleigh rolled his eyes.

"Not the Thanksgiving charades again, Belle." Marshall ducked his chin, shaking his head. "Please, spare us from pretending to be turkeys."

"Fine, although I still say you both did an excellent job." She studied her fingernails a moment, then clapped her hands. "I've got it! We'll play Thanksgiving Would You Rather."

Ainsley straightened, her heartbeat accelerating. This was more like it. They actually played games! This was going to be fun.

"I'll tell you what I'd rather." Raleigh kept his voice quiet as he held Grace. "I'd rather we didn't play games and watched football instead."

"Too bad." Belle blew him a kiss. Raleigh's eyes were full of love as he grinned.

Ainsley turned her concentration to Ben, who'd fallen asleep in her arms. For all Belle's faults, Ainsley had to give it to her—she didn't lack guts. In fact, Ainsley wouldn't mind having a little of her confidence when it came to men.

"Well, pretty mama, you're on my team, then." Raleigh's stare challenged Belle.

"You got it." Belle looked at Marshall, then Ainsley. "You two up for this?"

Marshall guffawed. "Oh, we're up to it, sis. Aren't we, Ainsley?"

She gulped and nodded. She hadn't thought she'd be paired with Marshall. A little competition between the men and the women would have suited her just fine.

Hopefully, the game didn't require much physical interaction. Marshall already appealed to her too much. Her whole life was wrapped up in Laramie, not with a cowboy in Sweet Dreams.

But what would be the harm of a little Thanksgiving fun?

* * *

Whose idea had this been again?

"One more round!" Belle insisted.

Marshall looked at his sister's laughing face and at Ainsley's perplexed expression and shook his head. He was glad Ainsley could see this side of his sister. The funny, confident side. They'd eaten pumpkin pie with gobs of whipped cream earlier, and daylight was beginning to fade.

"Come on, Marsh, you have to answer." Belle pointed to him. "Would you rather pluck a Thanksgiving turkey or sleep with a snake?"

"What kind of question is that?" Raleigh slung his arm over her shoulders. "No one wants to sleep with a snake."

"I would. I'd choose the snake any day." Marshall shuddered. "Raw poultry gives me the creeps."

"Okay, okay," Belle said when the laughter died, "Ainsley's turn."

Marshall couldn't wait to hear what question Raleigh and Belle came up with. Ainsley fiddled with the hem of her sweater. So far her answers had been enlightening, and he found himself wanting to know more about her.

Belle opened her hands. "Would you rather soak your feet in mashed potatoes or wash your face with gravy?"

Ainsley laughed and shook her head. "You don't really expect me to answer that, do you?"

"Rules are rules." Belle's eyes twinkled with mischief.

"Well, that's a hard one." She tapped her finger against her lips. "I guess I'd rather soak my feet in mashed potatoes. I think the gravy would destroy my complexion."

They all laughed.

"Okay, Ainsley, it's our turn." Marshall scooted closer to her on the couch and kept his voice quiet so Belle and Raleigh couldn't hear. "What should we ask?"

"Remember, it has to relate to Thanksgiving," Belle said loudly, leaning forward.

As if they needed the reminder. He almost glared at her, but he refrained.

"This one's for Raleigh, so we should make it cooking related," Ainsley said quietly. "Belle said he only grills."

"Got it!" Marshall lifted his index finger. He whispered the idea in Ainsley's ear. Her perfume suited her, and her soft hair brushed his cheek.

She nodded, her eyes wide. "Yes. Perfect."

"Would you rather cook a Thanksgiving feast early-settler style—no oven—or clean all the dishes afterward without modern conveniences?"

Raleigh frowned. "Cooking without an oven

would require an open fire. And I like tending fires. Doing dishes without dish soap or running water sounds rough. I'd take the cooking."

"What if you were cooking indoors where it was five hundred degrees?" Belle asked. "Didn't they have outbuildings they used for kitchens back then?"

"That changes things." He pretended to shiver. "Give me a trough and hot water and I'll do the dishes. I'm best outdoors."

Two of the babies started waking up. Ainsley excused herself to get the bottles. Marshall followed her.

"Are you enjoying yourself?" he asked.

"More than you know," she said. "This has been the best Thanksgiving…ever."

"Ever? Now I know you're joking." He scrambled to come up with an explanation, but one look in her earnest eyes told him he was wrong. She meant it. Didn't she have family? "It can't be the best."

"It can. And it is." She blinked those green-gold eyes his way. After warming two bottles, she handed them to Marshall. "Will you take these to Belle and Raleigh? I'll warm the other two up and be right there."

"It's getting late." He held the bottles but shifted from one foot to the other. "Why don't we take off? They can feed the quadruplets by themselves. Let's leave them to it."

She nodded. "Sure."

He studied her a moment. She seemed down all of a sudden. "Is something wrong?"

"No." She shook her head, her braid swishing behind her. "I was just thinking."

"About what?"

"I usually work through Thanksgiving Day."

"And we made you work today…" He wanted to kick himself. Why hadn't he told her she could have the day off?

"No, that's not what I'm saying." Her eyebrows furrowed together. "This was a real Thanksgiving. I wasn't waiting tables. I got to hold a baby and eat a fantastic dinner with great people. And I thoroughly enjoyed the games. Don't laugh, but I'm a little sad to see it end."

The fact she enjoyed his family as much as he did warmed him down to his toes.

"It doesn't have to end." He tilted his head. "We can stay here…"

"No, no, you're right. Let's give them some privacy."

He jutted his jaw out, an idea forming. "How about we snag a couple of pieces of pie and head back to my place for a while?"

She blinked, her face glowing. "I'd like that. Except, let's make it my place. I insist."

"Deal." He held up the bottles. "I'll drop these off and be back for the others lickety-split."

Her laugh filled the air, and he knew he was grinning like a fool but didn't care. He headed back to the living room, told Raleigh and Belle that he and Ainsley were taking off, and loped back to the kitchen as Ainsley finished heating the other bottles. He delivered them to the living room, as well.

A few minutes later, after thanking Belle for the mouthwatering meal and layering on their coats, Marshall escorted Ainsley out the back door to their cabins. He held a plate with two slices of pie. The weather was cold, the wind bitter, but he didn't mind. The faint glow of the sun on the horizon was all that remained of daylight.

"Are you sure you don't mind me coming over?" He glanced Ainsley's way. Her chin was tucked against the wind.

"I want you to."

Four simple words. That was all it took to put an extra spring in his step. *She wants me here.* He imagined this was how a teacher's pet felt or the guy who caught the eye of the homecoming queen in high school. Marshall had never been the teacher's pet or anyone's favorite. He wouldn't mind being Ainsley's.

They approached her cabin, and, after she unlocked it, he held the door open for her.

They hung up their coats and he jerked his thumb to the fireplace. "Want me to start a fire?"

"Yes, please. I'll put on a pot of coffee."

Within minutes, crackling sounds from the fire and the aroma of coffee filled the air. Ainsley tucked her feet under her body on the end of the couch, and Marshall sat on the other end. He tapped his jeans with his hand as one thought bothered him.

"Did we keep you from your family today?" he blurted out.

"What?" She frowned, then brightened. "No, not even close."

He knew so little about her, and he wanted to learn more. "You don't celebrate Thanksgiving with them?"

"I don't have much family." Her gaze was trained on the fireplace. "Mom left when I was younger. And I haven't seen my father in about three years. I never met my grandparents. I have no siblings."

"Why haven't you seen your dad?" He tried to add up her family situation, but no matter how he did, it wasn't a pretty picture.

"He's an alcoholic." She sighed, her chin dipping. "We had an unhealthy relationship."

"How unhealthy?"

She gave him a small smile. "Bad enough for me to walk away and never come back."

"Did he… Was he…" Marshall didn't know how to ask it. He worried she'd been abused.

"He was a drunk and he got mean sometimes, but my physical health wasn't in jeopardy, if that's what you're concerned about. We had a codependent relationship. And it was holding me back. Curdling my heart."

"I'm sorry, Ainsley."

"I am, too." She didn't seem eager to say any more about the topic. "What about you? I assume you and Belle have always spent the holidays together."

"I wish." He turned to stare at the fire once more. "We didn't see each other for five years when we were teens."

"That's awful! What happened?"

Emotion pressed against his chest. He didn't tell people about this part of his life. Sure, his best friends, Wade, Clint and Nash, knew, but… He snuck a peek at Ainsley. Her big eyes gleamed with compassion. He wanted her to know. Didn't need to keep it a secret.

"I grew up in Casper. Mom had a string of boyfriends who lived with us. Ed moved in when we were twelve. He was abusive. Mom didn't see it. Or she didn't want to see it. I don't know. I was stupid and thought she'd get a clue if I took matters into my own hands. The next year when she told us we were moving out of our apartment and into Ed's house, I told her I'd kill him first. Got a knife from the kitchen and everything. A week later I was sent to Yearling Group Home for teen boys here in Sweet Dreams. I never saw my mother again."

"Oh, Marshall. I'm so sorry." She sounded distraught, and her hand covered her chest. "What about Belle?"

He raked his fingers through his hair. "Within six months she had run away. It's a long story and not mine to tell, but Belle lived with a few foster families after that."

The fire crackled, warming the room.

"You wouldn't have killed him. She must have known that." Her stare held no judgment.

"I don't think of myself as a murderer, but, truthfully, I don't know. I hated Ed. Hated that I couldn't protect myself or my sister from him." He stood, stopping in front of the fireplace. "It's in the past, so I'm leaving it there. I'm sorry. I didn't mean to unload it on you. I figured we'd eat some pie and share happy stories."

Ainsley rose and joined him, setting her hand on his sleeve. "Don't apologize. I think we all have hard stuff in our pasts. At least you and Belle have each other now."

"Yeah, well, I still didn't mean to ruin your Thanksgiving."

"You didn't. I meant what I said earlier. This is the nicest Thanksgiving I can remember."

He looked at her beautiful face, glowing in the firelight, and wanted to pull her into his arms.

Holding her was one thing, but holding on to her was another. Whenever he tried to keep his loved ones safe and close by, he found a way to ruin it.

He stepped back. He was better off not getting too close. Then he'd have nothing to lose.

Chapter Five

"I'm desperate for supplies. Can we stop at the grocery store after church?" Ainsley was thankful Marshall had offered to drive her into town Sunday morning. His truck handled the high winds better than her small car. She peeked at him as they made the twenty-minute drive into Sweet Dreams. He had trimmed his scruff, and every now and then a whiff of his aftershave blew her way. The man smelled good.

This was the first time she'd ventured off the property since arriving. Not only did she need the peace of a worship service, she needed a break from living on the ranch. She hoped Marshall wouldn't be in a hurry to go back this afternoon.

"You got it. I'm running low, myself." He kept the heel of one hand on top of the steering wheel, while adjusting the heat settings with the other.

She hadn't seen him much in the few days since Thanksgiving, and she hadn't been able to get what he'd told her off her mind. At the time, she'd been trying to process what he was saying. Only later did the barrage of questions hit her. Like how could a mother send her son away to a group foster home and never see him again? Or defend a man abusing her children?

How could a mother walk away from her own kids and never look back?

She stared out the window at the open plains. She and Marshall had that in common. Both of their mothers had ditched them. Did his heart have scar tissue the way hers did?

"After the service, we can have breakfast at Dottie's Diner if you'd like." Marshall glanced at her. "I haven't been in to see her for a while."

"I'd like that. I've only met her once. She's a friend of my roommate's mother." The day was shaping up better than she'd hoped. Church. A hot meal in a restaurant. And stocking up on supplies. She really should pick up a few Christmas decorations, too. One thing she'd always insisted on was decking the halls with strand upon strand of Christmas lights and homemade gingerbread ornaments for the tree.

The gingerbread tradition had begun out of necessity when she was eleven. Her mother had left the previous summer, taking all the

Christmas decorations with her. Every last one. And with Dad drinking away their rent money, there'd been nothing to do but make decorations. The ranch cook where they'd been living had given Ainsley the recipe.

She'd made them every year since. They were her way of reminding herself Christmas would go on no matter what.

A small herd of wild horses huddling together in the distance caught her eye. Poor things. The cold wind would be brutal for any animal outside on a day like this. She snuggled into her scarf. At least she had a warm ride to church.

Main Street came into view, and Ainsley soaked the town in. Storefronts displayed Christmas decorations, and evergreen wreaths hung on doors and light posts. The word *charming* barely did the town justice.

"My friend Clint's wife, Lexi, owns that building." He pointed to the corner. Above the entrance in the brick, Department Store was spelled out.

"It doesn't look like a department store." She craned her neck to keep it in view as they passed by.

He chuckled. "It isn't. It's a banquet hall. She's a wedding planner."

A wedding planner? Sounded frilly and unrealistic. Fancy weddings were for people who led different lives, normal ones. Unlike her, those kind of people had dads to walk them down the aisle and grandparents who would beam with pride.

"What does Clint do?" She took note of the other stores. A barber, real estate agency, insurance company, coffee shop and jeweler all occupied the town.

"He runs Rock Step Ranch. It was passed down to Lexi from her father after he died." Marshall pointed to the other side of the street. "See Amy's Quilt Shop? My friend Nash married Amy the weekend Belle went into labor with the quadruplets."

She shifted in her seat. Marshall sure had a lot of friends nearby. She'd thought of him as a loner. Maybe she'd been wrong.

"My buddy Wade lives in the area, too, but he's about half an hour from Sweet Dreams, and his ranch is pretty secluded. Maybe you'll be able to meet some of them while you're here."

"Maybe." What would his friends think of her? She looked down at her long, puffy black jacket. She'd purchased it from a discount store on a 75 percent off clearance rack last spring. The dark gray slacks and burgundy sweater she'd bought at a thrift store for three bucks each. She didn't have much money for extras.

Oh, well. She'd lived this long without caring

about other people's opinions, so why should she start now?

Marshall turned down a side road, and within minutes they were walking toward the church entrance.

"What a lovely church." She stumbled on a crack in the pavement, and Marshall took her by the elbow to steady her. She murmured her thanks. The white siding and steeple looked picture-perfect.

"It is, isn't it?" He held the door open, and she swept past him. "I haven't been here in a while."

"Why not?" She couldn't imagine not attending church regularly.

"I've got responsibilities." He hung up his coat and reached for hers.

"Everyone has responsibilities." She handed him her coat. "What about priorities?"

"My priorities are Belle and the babies." They entered the worship area and found an empty pew near the middle.

"If God isn't number one in your life, something needs to change." As she flipped over the service handout, she wished she could take the words back. Who was she to lecture anyone on their faith? "I'm sorry, Marshall. I don't mean to sound so judgy."

"It's okay. I don't expect you to understand. Oh, hey, there's Clint and Lexi." He pointed to an attractive couple on the other side of the aisle. The slender woman had long, wavy brown hair, and the man next to her was tall with short brown hair. "Nash, Amy and Ruby are behind them to the left."

Another extremely good-looking couple, but this one had a young girl—a cute little blonde. "Who's Ruby?"

"Ruby is Nash's little sister, but he and Amy are raising her as their daughter."

Ainsley couldn't stop staring at the adorable child. She looked so cute putting stickers on a paper. Every now and then she would glance up at her dark-haired mommy with a big smile. The girl reminded Ainsley of herself at that age, except her mother and father never brought her to church.

"What about your other friend, Wade?" Ainsley looked around for a single man about Marshall's age. A few guys seemed to fit.

"I haven't seen Wade in church since we were at Yearling Group Home together."

Ainsley frowned. How sad. The pastor started the service then, and she got lost in the beautiful hymns and sermon.

A pause was taken for silent prayers. *Thank You, Lord, for the opportunity to take care of the quadruplets. Please open Marshall's friend*

Wade's heart to a relationship with You and bring Marshall to church regularly.

The need to pray for something else tugged on her subconscious.

She hadn't thought about nursing school or the hospital job in over a week. She could chalk it up to the unrelenting focus of caring for infants, but she refused to lie to herself. The babies weren't taking her mind off her goals. Marshall was.

She'd never had a male friend before. Eating dinner with him every night was not only relaxing, it was fun. They got along well. He was easy to talk to.

Face it, Ainsley, he's a distraction.

She'd worked too hard and for too long to let anything budge her from becoming a nurse. *Please let the hospital look at my application with favor so I can land the job. And let me be accepted into nursing school.*

As the service wrapped up, she felt confident God was holding her in His arms and steering her on the path she'd chosen after leaving her father. The people she'd loved might have let her down, but God wouldn't. God would never let her down.

Her thoughts turned to Belle, and she brought her hand to her heart, almost gasping.

She hadn't prayed for Belle—not once since she'd met her.

And who needed her prayers more than the mother of those dear babies?

Lord, please convince Belle to get the medical help she needs and fill her with the desire to mother the infants. And grant me patience with her.

She didn't want the quadruplets to grow up without a loving mother. If praying would change Belle's heart, she'd keep doing it. Gladly.

"It's good to see you, slick." Dottie Lavert set laminated menus on the table of the booth and turned to Ainsley. "How are the babies, peaches? I'm sure their mama appreciates the extra hands."

Marshall shook his head. He'd never understood Dottie's nickname for him. And where did *peaches* come from? He peeked at Ainsley. She did have a sweet, wholesome look about her. He certainly hoped Belle appreciated Ainsley's extra hands. He knew he did.

"The babies are really sweet." Ainsley's smile was bright and genuine. She didn't seem fazed by the nickname. She nodded to the menu. "What do you recommend?"

"What are you hungry for?" Dottie's silver hair was twisted up in the back, and poufy bangs curved over her forehead. She was a plump woman with a heart of gold. "The omelets will fill you right up, but the waffles will tickle your taste buds."

"I'll have the waffles." Ainsley snapped her menu shut.

He liked a woman who knew her mind. He smiled at Dottie. "And I'll have the Western omelet."

"Comin' right up." Dottie winked and left.

Ainsley tore two sugar packets and dumped them into her coffee. "Your friends all seemed nice."

Marshall had introduced her to them after church, and he was relieved Ainsley approved.

She stirred the sugar into the brew. "How long have Clint and Lexi been together?"

"About a year." He took a sip of the black coffee. Hot and strong, the way he liked it.

"Ruby is a cutie pie."

"She has us all wrapped around her little finger. It's good to see her so talkative."

"What do you mean?" Her eyebrows drew together.

"Before Ruby went to live with Nash and Amy, she'd been neglected. Nash hadn't known she existed."

"The poor, dear thing." Ainsley's tone reeled with anguish.

"Yeah, we're all happy she's here."

She got a faraway look in her eyes. "I looked

like her when I was little. Blond hair, skinny."
She dipped her chin for a moment. "Seeing her
brought back memories."

"Good ones?"

"Some." She wouldn't meet his gaze.

He wished all her memories were good. "And
the others?"

She gave her head a soft shake, her hair spill-
ing over her shoulders in the process.

"I'm sorry." He shouldn't have pressed her,
knowing she'd cut ties with her dad.

His own memories weren't worth dwelling on
either. He'd been such a naive kid. Why had he
ever believed his mom would stick up for them?
Best to shove his past in the back of his mind
where it belonged.

Dottie set enormous platters of food in front
of them. "One order of waffles and a Western
omelet. You kids holler if you need anything."

He looked around the retro diner with its vinyl
booths and stools, the long counter filled with
the Sunday crowd. The sound of conversations,
laughter and a cook barking out orders filled the
air. A place like this was no place to get stuck
in rotten childhood memories.

"It's our day off, and we're going to enjoy it."
He reached for the saltshaker. "Prepare yourself
for a stick-to-your-ribs breakfast. After that, I'll
take you wherever you'd like."

Her lips curved up. "Thanks, Marshall."

Hearing his name on her lips made his heart wobble. "You're welcome."

Wobbly hearts were no good. It meant he'd begun to care about her, and caring brought responsibilities. He couldn't be there for Ainsley *and* Belle, not when Ainsley planned on leaving in a few weeks.

Maybe it was good she had a life in Laramie that didn't include the quadruplets or him. Then he wouldn't have to make impossible decisions, and life would continue the way it was.

Sweet Dreams was messing with her head. The more time Ainsley spent with Marshall, the more she was losing her grip on her emotions.

She'd put her mother's abandonment behind her. She'd moved on from her guilt about her father. And she no longer thought about the little girl she'd been. So why were these issues bubbling up like the vinegar and baking soda volcano she'd made for the science fair as a kid?

"Here we are. It's not exactly a shopping mecca, but you should be able to find most of your list in here." Marshall pushed the shopping cart toward the produce aisle in Sweet Dreams Groceries. Ainsley stayed close to him. Her pants felt ready to burst from the delectable waffles she'd overindulged in. The breakfast she'd polished off an hour ago was the least of her problems, though.

Ainsley Draper did not mourn the lonely child she'd been. She didn't dwell on her father's problems. Not anymore. And she certainly didn't fall for caring, attractive cowboys who actually liked her enough to want to cheer her up.

Well, she'd never met a gorgeous cowboy who wanted to cheer her up before, so maybe that was part of the issue.

Your emotions don't control you, Ainsley. You control them. So take your shopping list out of your purse and get it together already!

After taking a deep breath, she calmly unfolded her list and started adding apples and navel oranges to the cart. When they finished selecting vegetables, they continued through the meat and dairy sections.

"I need to find the breakfast items and the baking section." She tried not to notice the man next to her, but something about his strong, calloused hands on the bar of the cart mesmerized her. The same hands that gently changed the babies' diapers also worked hard on a demanding ranch. Marshall had a quiet strength.

"Baking, huh?" He grinned her way. "Sounds good."

"It's not what you think." She walked tall, feeling brighter. "It's for my Christmas decorations."

"You bake your decorations?"

"Yes, I make gingerbread ornaments every year, and I'll be starting them this afternoon." She couldn't remember when she'd wanted to make them as much as she did now.

"You need some help?" He turned down the cereal aisle.

Did she need help? She almost laughed. She'd been making them on her own for thirteen years. No one had ever helped before.

The thought almost stopped her in her tracks.

No one had helped her because she'd had no one close enough to want to be involved. Her roommate, Tara Epworth, would have pitched in last year, but she worked full-time and went to school, leaving no hours for fun.

Did Ainsley want help? She shot him a sideways glance. "I'm sure you have better things to do."

He tossed a box of chocolate cereal in the cart. "Not really. Raleigh would love it if I was out riding pasture all day, but…"

She chuckled, then bit her lower lip. Maybe having a helper wouldn't be the worst thing.

"I don't blame you if you want to be alone." He stopped in front of the granola bars and searched for the box he wanted. He selected peanut butter with chocolate chips.

She debated how to answer.

"I've got things to catch up on, anyhow," he said, sounding regretful.

"Like what?" She tilted her head, watching his reaction.

He faced her and blinked. A sheepish grin spread across his face.

"I don't know. I'll think of something."

"Of course you can help." She waved his words away. "And in the meantime, I have a bunch of Christmas items I need to find."

"I think we'll find the Christmas stuff this way." He pointed to the left.

They wound their way through the store, and Ainsley filled the cart with two boxes of white Christmas lights, a tabletop artificial tree, candy canes, sparkly white ribbon and an inexpensive silver star for the tree topper.

When they'd checked out, they loaded their goodies into Marshall's truck and hopped inside to escape the wind. Ainsley blew on her hands as Marshall started the vehicle and reached behind her headrest to back out of the spot. His wrist was close to her cheek. Her pulse took off.

This wasn't just a friend she'd been hanging out with. Marshall was an attractive man—not only physically but inside, as well. She shouldn't have told him he could help. Wasn't she supposed to be focused on her agenda? The one where she drove off at the end of December, got the job in the ICU and hunkered down to get her nursing degree?

Well, one afternoon wouldn't destroy her plans.

At least, she hoped it wouldn't.

If she was wrong, something told her making gingerbread decorations with Marshall this afternoon would be the best mistake she ever made.

Chapter Six

Fifteen minutes—he'd pop in and check on Belle and the babies for fifteen minutes—that was it. Marshall hurried along the path to the main house. Ainsley had said they needed Sundays off, and he agreed. But this wasn't breaking the rules; this was visiting his loved ones. Wasn't that what people did on their days off? And, anyway, he had an entire hour before Ainsley expected him at her cabin. Earlier he'd helped unload her supplies and promised to come back at four so she could have some time to herself before they baked.

He was more excited about the prospect than he cared to admit.

Spending time with Ainsley filled an emptiness he hadn't been aware of before she'd arrived on the ranch. He'd never thought of himself as lonely, but maybe he hadn't realized it. It made sense. He'd been living with Belle in Cheyenne since they'd turned eighteen. Three years ago, after Belle and Raleigh had married and Belle moved to Sweet Dreams, Marshall's social calendar had emptied. Since then, Decembers had been low on the holiday cheer scale for him. If it hadn't been for his job in Cheyenne, he probably would have moved back to Sweet Dreams sooner.

After two knocks on the back door, Marshall let himself in and headed to the living room. Raleigh was kneeling on the floor, changing Grace's diaper. Lila grunted in her bouncy seat, and Ben fussed in discomfort.

"Hey, Raleigh, how are the munchkins doing?" Marshall bent to pick up Ben, who was about to cry. Cradling the boy, he tapped his nose. "You don't need to cry, cowboy. Uncle Marsh has you."

"How does it look like they're doing?" Raleigh snapped, glaring up at him. "Her diaper leaked, and I've gone through half a box of wipes trying to clean it up." He waved toward the pile of used wipes next to him. "I don't care if this outfit can be saved. I'm trashing it."

Marshall pressed his lips together to keep from laughing. Raleigh's face had grown brick red, and his jerky movements were clearly not soothing Grace, who squirmed beneath his touch.

"Want me to get another outfit for her?" Holding Ben in one arm, he nodded in the direction of the bedroom.

"What I want is for my wife to get out of bed. It's bad enough I'm up half the night with these four—I can't do this all day Sunday, too. I've got cattle to feed. Fence to check. Need to see if a heifer is acting suspicious today…" Raleigh unfolded a fresh diaper and tucked it under Grace. In his haste he ripped the sticker tab off the diaper. "I can't do this anymore!" Raleigh abruptly stood and marched out of the room. The slam of the back door echoed in Marshall's ears.

What had just happened? He looked down at Grace, sucking on her fist and happily kicking her bare legs in the air. Lila continued to grunt. Ben wasn't crying, but he was squirmy and unhappy. Max sat there taking it all in. Marshall let out a long sigh and went to the babies' room for a new outfit for Grace. Then he laid Ben down next to her. The boy didn't like that and let out a howl. Marshall rolled him onto his tummy, and he immediately quieted.

After putting a new outfit on Grace, Marshall changed Lila. Max was fine, but Ben got cranky at the tummy time, so Marshall strapped him and the girls back into their bouncy seats. In the kitchen, he found the feeding chart. The last entry had been by Ainsley at 5:00 p.m. yesterday.

A burst of annoyance shot through his brain. Ainsley had gone to the trouble of creating these charts to make life easier on Raleigh and Belle, yet neither of them could be bothered to use them? And big deal Raleigh had to change a particularly nasty diaper. Marshall and Ainsley had done the same thing countless times. Neither of them had run out the door. Talk about immature.

He dug his cell phone out of his pocket and dialed Raleigh. No answer.

Irritation spiraled through his body, tensing his muscles. He could text Raleigh, but what would be the point?

Then another thought occurred. If Raleigh didn't come back, who would take care of the children?

Marshall looked at the bedroom door where Belle had undoubtedly locked herself away. His irritation turned into full-blown anger.

This was *his* day off.

Marshall had a date—*er, appointment*—to help Ainsley bake gingerbread, and he would be there at four even if it meant dragging his sister out of bed and riding out to pasture to lasso Raleigh himself.

No more Mr. Nice Guy.

He quickly warmed four bottles and returned to the living room. It took a minute to prop the bottles for all the babies. Then he strode down the hall and knocked firmly on Belle's door. Once. Twice.

No answer.

He pounded on it. "Belle, open up!"

"What?" She cracked the door and glared. "What's the problem?"

"The problem is your husband ran off to pasture and left me to watch the babies."

"So?"

He wanted to push the door open but refrained. "So, it's my day off. Now get out here."

"Don't tell me what to do." Her biting tone usually made him back down.

"Don't treat me like your servant."

She opened the door wide as her chin rose to its haughtiest level. "How dare you."

"How dare *you*." He widened his stance, glowering at her.

"Me? What have I done?"

"Nothing. And that's the problem." He took in the dark spots under her eyes and the lines around her mouth. Worry lines. He wiped his forehead with the back of his hand. "Come out here and take care of them."

"By myself?" She looked at him as if he'd suggested skydiving without a parachute.

"Why not?" He'd been doing it. Ainsley had been doing it. Even Raleigh had been doing it. Why couldn't his sister—the babies' mother—

watch them on her own? Ainsley's warning came to mind. "I think your sister has postpartum depression...nothing to mess around with..."

He instantly deflated. "Belle, when's your next doctor's appointment?"

Her gaze fell to the floor. "I don't know."

"Why don't you make one?"

"I don't need to see a doctor." She wouldn't look him in the eye.

"You had quadruplets. I'm sure things are out of whack."

"Well, my body is, that's for sure."

"Do you think it could be more than physical?" He cringed, hoping she'd take the hint without blowing up.

"I'm not a mental case if that's what you're implying." Two red splotches spread on her cheeks.

"I would never imply that. But Ainsley mentioned postpartum depression..."

"Ainsley?" She stepped toward him, getting in his face. "What does she know about anything? It's none of her business. And last I checked she doesn't have kids, so why are you listening to her anyhow?"

"Something's not right, Belle," he said softly. "A doctor could help."

"If you want to help, then find Raleigh and tell him to get back here."

He hated when she acted like this. So stubborn. The ticking of the clock reminded him of his *appointment* with Ainsley. He checked his watch. Four on the dot.

What was he supposed to do? Leave the babies with Belle and hope she'd take an interest in them until Raleigh decided he'd checked enough of the cattle to come back? Or call Ainsley and tell her he'd have to skip the gingerbread decorations?

He didn't want to skip it.

He wanted to run out the back door and down the path to Ainsley's cabin. It had been a couple of hours since he'd sat next to her on the pew at church. He'd felt more peaceful there than he had in a long time.

God, why does this keep happening? I keep getting stuck with the job of babysitting. I love my nieces and nephews, but this is too much. Belle and Raleigh are more than capable of handling these infants. What should I do?

The house was quiet. The babies would more than likely fall asleep soon. He wouldn't be putting them in danger by leaving Belle with them. And it wouldn't hurt her to spend the afternoon with them by herself.

He pulled his shoulders back and gave his sister a curt nod. "They're taking their bottles now. They've all been changed. You'll be fine."

"But, Marshall!"

Pivoting, he marched down the hallway, paused to smile at the quads all nestled in their seats and continued through the breezeway and out the door.

Taking his phone out of his pocket, he texted Raleigh. Babies are changed and fed. Belle's alone with them. See you tomorrow.

Shoving the phone back in his pocket, he began to whistle as he ambled down the lane. It smelled like a snowstorm was coming—the ideal time to build a fire in the fireplace and bake some gingerbread with his pretty neighbor.

Sundays off were a good thing indeed.

"I'll have to let you go soon. Marshall will be here any minute." Ainsley propped the phone between her cheek and shoulder as she gathered the baking supplies. She'd called her roommate, Tara Epworth, and had lost track of time.

She still wasn't convinced letting Marshall help with the gingerbread was the right move. What if something happened and her tradition was ruined?

Her father had ruined more traditions than she cared to remember.

"Oh, that's fine," Tara's cheerful voice rang loudly. "Just promise me you'll stick to your rules. No unpaid overtime. Sundays off. And don't let the mother belittle you or treat you bad. You're doing her the favor."

Ainsley chuckled. "I know, I know. I keep telling myself the same thing."

"Is there anything I can do?"

"Actually, yes, there is something you can do. Will you pray for Belle? I'm convinced she has postpartum depression." Ainsley didn't worry about Tara's reaction to prayer since they went to church together whenever possible. Tara always had her back, and Ainsley was thankful for her friendship.

"Of course I will! See? This is why I love you, Ainsley. You could be counting the minutes until you can squeal your tires out of that place, but instead you're willing to pray for her."

Ainsley blinked away the emotion Tara's words brought up. "You'd do the same."

"No, I wouldn't. I'd tell her off and leave her to figure it out on her own. And, for the record, that would not be the right move. But I'd still do it."

Ainsley laughed. Two raps on the front door almost made her drop the phone.

"He's here. I've got to go."

"Okay, tell that hunky cowboy hello for me."

"I did not say he was hunky." Ainsley shook her head as her neck burst into flame.

"You implied it."

"Oh, stop! I'll talk to you soon."

"Bye!"

Ainsley tossed the phone onto the counter and let Marshall inside. His nose was red as he hung up his coat.

"You look happy and cold. Were you out and about on the ranch?" She returned to the counter, where she'd lined up sugar, flour, molasses and other ingredients for the cookies.

"You could say that."

"I thought I saw Raleigh on horseback a little while ago, but I must have mixed you two up." She pulled cookie sheets out of the cupboard and set them next to the stove. "He's likely helping Belle."

Marshall scratched his chin. He had *guilty* stamped all over him. What was going on?

"No, you saw Raleigh. I popped in for a few minutes to check on the babies, and he threw a hissy fit and left."

Why was Marshall going over there on a Sunday? Her internal warning system moved up from green to yellow. Had Belle asked him to check on the babies? Hadn't Ainsley talked to him about this already?

Her father's empty promises ran through her mind like a highlight reel of the Wyoming Cowboys' college football game.

Marshall padded to the kitchen, turning on the faucet to wash his hands. The tight quarters didn't help her mood. His sleeve brushed her arm and she almost jumped. *Don't lose your cool, Ainsley. Stay calm.*

"Who is watching the babies?" She used her least threatening tone. "You said Raleigh left."

"They're fine." He wiped his hands on the dish towel.

She had a vision of all four babies wailing in the living room while Belle hid behind the locked door of her bedroom.

"Marshall." She captured his gaze with her own. "Who is watching them?"

Worry and guilt flitted through his expressive dark brown eyes. "Belle is."

"For how long?" She still didn't have much confidence in his sister at this point.

He shrugged. "Raleigh needed to check the cattle. He'll be back soon."

She found the mixing bowls and made space for them on the small counter. Why was she nervous about the situation? It's what she'd wanted. Expected. Belle was taking care of her babies. Raleigh had been there earlier. And Marshall was taking the day off.

So why did it feel wrong?

He rubbed his hands together. "What do we do first?"

She wouldn't be able to enjoy herself if she didn't ask one more question. "Are you positive your sister is okay with the babies by herself right now?"

His face fell as he shrugged. "Honestly? I don't know. But I texted Raleigh. And they'd all been changed and fed before I left, so I'm hoping for the best."

She exhaled in relief. Why had she worried? Of course Marshall hadn't walked out and left the babies screaming or starving. He'd thought enough to text Raleigh, too. He was responsible. Trustworthy.

"I'm sorry, Marshall. I shouldn't have doubted you."

His throat worked before he replied. "I doubt myself all the time."

"You shouldn't."

Inches separated them, and she felt drawn to this man. His eyes darkened and his lips parted slightly. The moment took on a life of its own. Keeping an emotional distance had never been difficult for her.

Until now.

And she didn't like it. Didn't like being attracted to him. Didn't like being vulnerable.

But she liked the alternative even less.

Being vulnerable meant her heart was still beating.

She accepted she had a bond with him whether

she wanted it or not. She just hoped it wouldn't interfere with her real life in Laramie.

"Are they burning? It smells like char." Marshall cracked a window open, but the snow he'd predicted earlier instantly flooded in, so he slammed it shut. The past couple of hours had been fun. After confessing to Ainsley he'd left Belle with the kids, she'd dropped her worried demeanor and directed him to pour ingredients into the bowl. A flour fight had ensued—the smudge on her cheek looked cute—then they'd chilled the dough before rolling out part of it. Most of the cookies had been baked. One batch of gingerbread men was in the oven, and Marshall was supposed to be cutting out cookies shaped like houses with the remains of the dough.

"They don't look burnt. Something must have dripped in the oven the last time it was used." She sprinkled flour on the rolling pin and resumed spreading out the dough.

If he ignored the burnt-toast smell, the aroma of cinnamon and cloves clung to the air.

"Okay, cut these out," she said. "I'll spread more wax paper on the table for the cookies to cool."

"Got it." He wanted to nudge his elbow into her side, get her to laugh, but he obeyed orders.

He liked watching her bake. She followed each direction on the recipe precisely. No haphazard tearing of the wax paper for her. She ripped it down in one straight line and carefully flattened it on the table. Her lips were pursed as she stood back and checked it. She adjusted one corner slightly and came back to stand next to him.

"You can get more cookies out of this dough if you press the cutter a little closer to the edge."

He held back a laugh. "A little closer, huh? Why don't you show me?" He handed her the cutter and leaned back a fraction. Shameless of him to want her near him. When she bent to cut out the house, he inhaled the faded scent of her perfume.

"Don't forget to make the little hole for the ribbon." Using a knife, she ground out a small hole in the corner of the house. Straightening, she smiled, clearly satisfied with the end result. "I'd better check on the ones in the oven."

"What happens next?" He continued cutting out dough while she set the hot baking sheet on top of the stove to cool.

She glanced at the clock. "It's about suppertime. I can make us sandwiches if you'd like."

"How about we throw a frozen pizza in the oven after this batch?"

She nodded. "Yes, please."

"And we can put a Christmas movie on while we eat."

"Okay, I *love* the way you're thinking," she said. "And then I'll mix up the royal icing and, if you want to stay, you can help decorate them. Or if you're tired, I understand."

"I'm not a quitter." He waggled his eyebrows. "Just don't get mad if I sneak a little of the icing."

"I'll look the other way. Let me get the new batch in the oven, and I'll clean up."

"And I'll grab that pizza. Be right back." He put on his boots and went outside. Snow continued to fall in the darkness. Looked like he'd be shoveling in the morning. He didn't mind. The frigid air added a spring to his step. He loved the crisp freshness of Wyoming in December.

Letting himself into his cabin, he paused. He hadn't thought about Belle or Raleigh or the babies since he and Ainsley started making the cookies. He checked his phone. Four texts from Belle. One from Raleigh.

Worry clenched his stomach. What if something had happened to the children and he'd ignored Belle—for what?—to make cookies?

He quickly read the texts. The ones from Belle were all variations on the same theme. She was exhausted and needed help. One of the babies was making weird noises and she didn't know what to do. Usually, guilt and anxiety ate him up at the messages, but a strange sense of calm had taken over earlier and pushed out the guilt. Babies made noises sometimes. She'd be okay. And so would they.

Raleigh's made him frown. No apology. Just K.

Huh. K?

Maybe he should text them both and make sure everything was fine…

His phone dinged, and he almost dropped it. Had Belle been reading his mind? He checked the screen and let out a sigh of relief. Ainsley.

She wanted to know if he could bring over a pizza cutter. She didn't have one.

Why, yes I can. I'll be happy to eat pizza and watch movies with you. No drama. No babies interrupting the meal. No sister on an emotional roller coaster. And no brother-in-law barking at me.

Minutes later, he returned to Ainsley's. She'd stacked all the cookies in a rectangular container on the counter. The bowls and measuring spoons had disappeared, leaving clean, shiny surfaces in their place. She beamed at him. "What movie do you want to watch?"

"I don't know. Do you have a favorite?" He handed her the pizza cutter.

"I like to watch *Christmas Vacation*." She had a dreamy look on her face. "I always wondered what it would be like to grow up in a big house with a family like that, you know?"

He nodded thoughtfully. "Yeah, I do know. How old were you when your mom left?"

"Eleven." She found a pizza pan and set it on the counter. "It was June. She'd been telling Dad for months she'd leave if he didn't get his act together. She finally made good on her threats."

"What happened to make her leave?" Marshall unwrapped the frozen pizza and put it on the pan. His heartbeat started racing the way it did whenever he sensed danger or bad news. Funny how even grown up, he couldn't shake the fear.

"The usual." She leaned against the counter with her arms folded over her chest. "He'd emptied their bank account, disappeared for two days and waltzed in the door like nothing had happened."

Why did her explanation relieve him? He'd feared…the worst. That Ainsley's dad had been a horrible person like Ed.

"Mom didn't yell at him. She was calm as could be. I think something had died inside her long before then. She looked at me and said, 'Him or me? I'm heading out the door, and I'm never coming back.' I didn't know what to do. The question was impossible. I loved my dad. I knew he had a drinking problem, but I also knew he cared about me getting good grades and took me out riding when he was sober. Mom never had time for any of that."

"Makes sense."

She shook her head slightly, a tendril of hair dropping across her face. She pushed it behind her ear. "I didn't choose to stay with him because he was a great father or because my mom wasn't a caring mother."

"I'm not following." His gut told him he wasn't going to like what he was about to hear.

Her sad eyes pierced him. "I knew he needed someone to take care of him. I couldn't imagine what would happen to him if I left, too."

Marshall rocked back on his heels, understanding flashing like lightning through his core. He let her words and their meaning sit there a minute. She'd loved her father and willingly stayed with him to take care of him, even though she'd been a child. The price she'd paid was high—her mother.

"I would have done the same thing, Ainsley."

"I know you would have," she whispered.

"How do you know?" He approached her, touching her arm. "I told you how I threatened Ed."

"Because you were willing to take that chance if it would have protected Belle. You couldn't have known your mother wouldn't believe you. You had no way of knowing she'd banish you."

Banished. Yes, that summed it up.

"She didn't want to believe me." He dropped his hand, but Ainsley grabbed it.

"Whatever happened wasn't your fault. Your mom didn't protect you or your sister, so you were put in the role."

"I couldn't protect Belle anymore when I was sent to Yearling Group Home. It was hours from where they lived. Do you have any idea how many times I tried to run away to help her? We were going to disappear together."

"I thought you said she did run away."

"She did. I think Ed had finally pushed her too far, and she was tired of living in fear. When she moved into her first foster home, she made me promise to stay put. She said she was fine and that the instant we turned eighteen, we'd have each other's backs for good."

The timer dinged. Ainsley turned and took the cookies out of the oven before sliding the pizza in their place.

"What happened when you turned eighteen?" Her eyes shimmered with compassion.

"We moved to Cheyenne. Got jobs at fast-food joints and rented an apartment together. Best years of my life."

Ainsley smiled. "I love hearing happily-everafters. Let's take this to the couch while the pizza cooks."

He sat in the recliner while she tucked one leg under the other on the couch.

"What about you?" he asked. "What happened after your mom left?"

Her eyebrows drew together. "Without my mother's income, we couldn't pay the bills. So we moved around the state. Dad worked as a cowboy for hire at several ranches. I grew up. Graduated from high school. Worked at day care centers, waited tables. Wanted to go to college. But…"

"Who would take care of your dad?"

"Right." She sighed. "Three years ago, he took a credit card out in my name without my knowledge. Maxed it out. I'd been saving to take online courses, and I had to use every penny and then some to pay the card off. I screamed at him. He didn't even remember doing it. I shut down. Just completely shut down. I was done. I knew if I didn't leave, I'd never have the kind of life I wanted. So I packed my stuff and drove to Laramie. I enrolled in the university. Left my dad my cell number and sent him a forwarding address and haven't heard from or seen him since."

He stood, crossing over to her, and held out his hand. She took it. He helped her to her feet and put his arms around her. "I'm sorry, Ainsley. I'm sorry you went through all that."

Her cheek lay against his chest, and he wanted to keep her in his arms indefinitely. He wanted to wipe away the pain of her past. But he couldn't even wipe away his own.

"Thanks," she whispered. She eased out of his arms and retreated to the kitchen. "I'll get the plates."

Get the plates? He followed her, confused by her abrupt change in topic.

He treaded gently. "I've never seen my mom again either."

"Yeah, I found out later mine had already started seeing someone else before she left us." She flashed him a fake smile. "I heard she remarried and moved to Utah."

"Ouch. Who do you have?" Marshall asked. "You know…who can you rely on?"

She faced him then. "God. I can always rely on God. And my roommate, Tara, is my best friend. I don't know what I would do without her."

God. Didn't surprise him. Ainsley lived her faith. For a moment, he envied it about her. He turned to his faith when it was convenient. How many times had he run from God? Blamed Him for life not turning out the way he'd wanted? He only prayed when he needed something.

"Ainsley?"

"Hmm?"

"Do you still want to watch the movie? I feel bad for bringing up all these painful memories."

"Of course I want to watch it. It makes me laugh. Gives me hope. Makes me believe my Christmas dreams exist, if that makes sense."

"And what are your Christmas dreams?" He strained for her answer. But she shook her head.

"They don't matter. I take life one dream at a time. I'm glad to be here with the babies. And after Christmas my real dreams will begin. I want the job in the ICU. Then, hopefully, I'll get into the nursing program. Everything else is icing on one of these gingerbread cookies."

Why he felt let down, he couldn't say. Maybe he'd hoped he could play a small part in her Christmas dreams.

He almost snorted. They barely knew each other. He must be losing it.

"And now I get to ask if you have any Christmas dreams of your own." Her face glowed.

"Nah. I'm living the dream." If only he believed it, he might not want more. "Well, I would like to sneak one of those cookies after we ice them."

She laughed, the sound joyous and tinkling. "I think I can arrange that. You sure you're up for decorating ornaments?"

"I'm up for it. But first, I'll get the movie ready."

Spending the afternoon and evening with Ainsley was all the Christmas dream he needed. Dreams never worked out all that great for him anyhow. But if he did have one, it would be for this time with Ainsley to last.

Wanting more was a dangerous thing. It was safer to be content with what he had.

Chapter Seven

❧

Ainsley slipped out of her boots in the main house the following Friday morning. The babies were starting to stir and the rest of the house was quiet. Today she was flushing Belle out of her room and keeping her out. Ainsley would walk her through all the baby care even if it meant taking the bedroom door off the hinges… Well, that was extreme. No taking doors off hinges.

The routine comforted her. She truly was blessed the babies had taken to the schedule so well. If only the adults on the ranch would get with the program…

She had assumed Raleigh was getting up sometime in the early-morning hours with the babies to feed them since the infants typically grew hungry later in the morning. However, all week Ainsley had watched Marshall hurry up the path to the house at 5:00 a.m. She'd first caught him doing it on Monday. The wind had woken her out of her slumber and she hadn't been able to get back to sleep. She'd finally given up and gone into the living room to read the Bible. She'd peeked out the window to see if fresh snow had fallen, and there Marshall was, chin tucked into the collar of his jacket, hands jammed into his pockets as he strode along the path. When they'd eaten dinner that night, she'd almost asked him about it, but something held her back.

Out of curiosity she began setting her alarm to go off before five. Every day he headed up to the main house. Why wouldn't he let Raleigh or Belle handle the children? And what else was he keeping a secret?

The upside to her new wake-up time was she'd carved out a special hour to study the Bible and pray. The early session centered her and let her fully enjoy her morning coffee. In fact she'd had three cups this morning in preparation for her mission.

"Belle?" She strode straight to her bedroom door and knocked. "I need to show you something."

They had less than thirty minutes before the babies would get fussy. She knocked again.

"Belle, wake up. Can you come out here?"

The door opened a sliver. "What do you want?"

"You!" She plastered on her happiest smile. "Throw on some sweats and join me. I'd like to show you something."

"Can't it wait?"

Ainsley wouldn't get annoyed. No sirree, she would not. "Nope."

"Fine. I'll be right out."

"Good," Ainsley said. "Want a cup of coffee?"

"Yes, please."

"Cream or sugar?"

"Both. Lots of both."

"You got it." Ainsley went to the kitchen, popped a pod into the Keurig and set a cute pink mug under it. Humming to herself, she reviewed the baby charts from yesterday. No new entries. As usual.

It was time to change that. She studied the counter—used bottles from last night had been carelessly strewn about. The bin of binkies was half-full. Normally, she'd do a quick spin around the living room, picking up pacifiers, burp cloths and such. Then she'd clean any dirty bottles and prepare a full day's worth before getting the babies out of their cribs.

But today she was waiting for Belle. Christmas was a few weeks away. Ainsley wasn't doing the new mom any favors by shielding her from the reality of baby care.

Three more minutes ticked by. *You're not escaping me this time, Belle Dushane.*

Ainsley poured cream and sugar into Belle's mug and marched back to the bedroom door. "Coffee's ready, Belle."

One one thousand. Two one thousand. Three one thousand. Four...

The door opened and Belle came out. Her thick black hair was pulled back in a ponytail, her face was scrubbed clean and she wore a loose-fitting long-sleeve T-shirt with black yoga pants. She looked young and pretty. Ainsley ignored her stony expression.

"How do you manage to look so cute in the morning? I resemble a ratty old stuffed animal. Never mind. I'm going to walk you through the morning prep." Ainsley extended her arm for Belle to lead the way. She didn't trust that the woman wouldn't escape if left to her own devices. "Your coffee is on the counter."

"Thanks." In the kitchen, Belle lifted the mug. "Why haven't you gotten the babies up?"

"I'm glad you asked," Ainsley said brightly. "I don't get them up before they awake. We're so blessed the little ones took to the schedule."

Belle frowned, sipping her coffee.

"When I arrive each morning, I spend five minutes tidying the living room. Then I come in here and wash any dirty bottles as well as the binkies. Would you grab the canister of formula and bring it over?"

Ainsley was on pins and needles waiting for her response. But Belle brought the formula over. Ainsley set the bin containing all the clean bottles on the counter. Then she washed her hands.

"I always make six bottles for each baby. As you know, Ben gets red, Max gets blue, Grace gets green and Lila gets yellow." She held up the bottom of four bottles so Belle could see the color markings. "I fill them with water to this line, then pour the scoops of formula in. You just screw the nipple on and shake for several seconds. Then I repeat until they're all ready. Stick them in the fridge and you're good to go. Here, you try."

Belle took a bottle, started filling it with water and held it up. "Is this enough?"

"Um, a little more. Try to get it to the line. It doesn't have to be perfect." Ainsley wanted to pinch herself. Belle was actually out here, making bottles! "Yep, now pour the scoops in. That's right. Here's a nipple." She held out the small plastic bin. Belle selected one. "Shake."

Belle shook it for a while. "That's it?"

"Easy-peasy." She nodded. "Let's knock the rest out. It only takes a few minutes."

Together they filled the rest of the bottles and lined them in the fridge. Then Ainsley took the chart over to the dining table. Belle followed, grunting as she sat in a chair. She continued drinking her coffee.

"The babies seem to be doing well on the four-hour rotation. When they get bigger, they'll sleep for longer stretches at night but you'll want to keep feeding them every four hours during the day. As they grow, they'll need more ounces at each feeding, too."

"Shouldn't we get them up?" Belle's forehead furrowed.

She couldn't believe Belle was finally showing some interest in them. *Thank You, Lord!*

"They aren't crying. They're safe in their beds. Right now it's important to prepare for the day." She slid the feeding chart to face Belle. "After each feeding session, I mark how many ounces they ate. See how Lila has a three in this box? She drank three ounces. It will help you monitor their habits."

"Oh, I get it. Then there's proof they're actually eating."

"Exactly. When you're done with your coffee, I'll show you my diaper tricks. I have a portable changing area on the floor so I don't have to leave them alone. Oh, I give them tummy time a few times a day, too. Not much, just a few minutes, but it's good for strengthening their little backs and necks. Don't ever leave them alone when they're on their stomachs, though."

Belle turned to look out the back window and took a long drink of her coffee. "Thank you for…this."

Belle was thanking her? Ainsley's heart melted. "You're welcome. Thank you for letting me spend time with your precious babies every day."

"They are precious, aren't they?" Belle's eyes grew watery.

"The most precious darlings I've ever seen."

She swiped under her eyes. "I'm going to start exercising and eating better. It will give me the energy to take care of them."

Ainsley didn't respond. Did Belle really think her problem was a lack of energy? She debated whether to mention seeing a doctor or keep her mouth shut.

She'd never been good at silence.

"Exercise is very therapeutic. Maybe you could talk to your doctor about appropriate workouts for this stage of being a mom."

"I don't need to see a doctor. I can walk on the treadmill."

Ainsley wasn't going to argue. "Good plan."

A few minutes ticked by in silence. She should start getting the babies up, but she feared it would send Belle back to her room.

"I love this time of year." Belle faced her suddenly. "I feel so cooped up, though. It's hard to get motivated."

"You probably haven't left the house much, have you?" She'd go stir-crazy in Belle's shoes.

"No."

She thought of Raleigh and Belle—how they had flashes of tender moments but far too many tense ones. Maybe they needed some time out of the house to reconnect.

"I have an idea. What if you and Raleigh went into town tomorrow, just the two of you?"

A smile lit Belle's face but dimmed as quickly. "I don't think he'd tear himself away from this place. Gotta work those cattle, you know."

Ainsley chuckled. "He's a rancher. That's what they do. I think he'd jump at the chance to do some Christmas shopping and have some alone time with you, though."

"You think?" Belle looked so forlorn, Ainsley almost jumped up to hug her.

"I do. I think you both need it. I'll watch the babies until you return. You two go and make a day of it and don't worry about hurrying back."

"You'd do that? Even after…"

"I told you. I love the babies. I'm happy to watch them. It will make me even more glad to watch them knowing you and Raleigh are keeping your marriage strong."

One of the infants let out a cry.

"Well, we'd better move. Let's get them up. I'll show you how to put fresh diapers and clothes on quadruplets in ten minutes flat."

"Ten minutes?" Belle arched one eyebrow. "I don't believe you."

"Time me." She grinned.

Yesterday, if anyone would have told her she'd have a decent conversation with Belle and make progress with her regarding the care of the quadruplets, she wouldn't have believed them. The crazy thing was she could see herself becoming friends with Belle in different circumstances. Maybe things were finally getting better.

She hoped so. There weren't many days left for Ainsley on the ranch. She wanted the babies to have a wonderful life with a mom who adored them and a dad who did, too. Thanksgivings with games and laughter. Christmases full of love. The things she'd missed out on as a child. Hopefully, this was a start.

He had to stop taking the early-morning shift with the babies.

Marshall heaved a bale of straw into the stall and poked it with a pitchfork. Just because Raleigh was used to heading out to the stables at 4:30 a.m. didn't mean his schedule was set in stone. Shouldn't *he* be feeding the babies at five instead of Marshall? He was their daddy, after all.

Marshall spread the straw around with the pitchfork, then leaned against the handle. The five o'clock feedings weren't bothering him as much as his conscience was. He'd told Ainsley he wouldn't go over at night to help anymore. And he didn't. Technically, he went over in the morning. The dark, quiet hours. Why? Because Belle was already waking up for the 1:00 a.m. feeding, and he wanted her rested so she could do more during the day.

But it felt sneaky. Underhanded.

Boots clomping on the hard dirt outside drew his attention. One of the ranch hands, Colby, stood in the doorway listening to Raleigh give him instructions. Then Colby left, and Raleigh continued to his office.

Marshall hung the pitchfork on a hook on the wall and went straight to Raleigh's office. He was sitting on a stool, looking over an invoice.

"Got a minute?" he asked.

"What's up?" Raleigh waved him in.

Marshall leaned against the doorjamb. A voice inside warned him to proceed cautiously. "Do you think you could have Colby or Dave start the morning chores instead of you?"

"Why?" Raleigh spun to face him, his legs wide, his hands lightly clasped together. "You know I'm in charge here. I have to check the outfit."

"I know you do." He didn't understand Raleigh's passion for looking over each cow. Yes, it had to be done, but Raleigh acted like the cattle would vanish in a poof if he wasn't out there riding every morning. He swallowed. "I've been going over at five to help feed the babies, and, while I like that it gives Belle a break, I feel like it's your place to feed them, not mine."

Raleigh stood, tucked his lips under and cocked his head. "You think it gives *Belle* a break, do you?"

"Well, yeah. Of course." He straightened, standing with his hips apart.

"Tell me, Marshall, when doesn't Belle have a break from feeding the babies?"

"I'm not going over there at midnight or one anymore, so she's—"

"Not getting up with them. I am." He jabbed his thumb into his own chest, and his voice rose. "And I'm giving them their bottles before bed, too. So forgive me if I'm not as worried about Belle needing a break as you are."

He bristled for a moment, then slumped. Why had he assumed Belle was handling the babies now that he'd stopped coming around every night?

Because it's easier to believe than the truth, dummy.

"And I'm sorry, Marshall, but I have a real problem with you sticking your nose into my business. I agreed to let you work here out of respect for Belle. I'm tired of you coddling her. And I'm tired of you running up to the house every afternoon to make googly eyes at the baby nurse. But most of all, I'm fed up with you interfering with my marriage!"

Let him work there? Marshall was the one doing *him* the favor, not the other way around.

"I don't coddle my sister, and I'm only running up to the house to help with the little ones. I've never interfered with your marriage." His blood boiled, and the more he thought about it, the more he wanted to grab his keys and leave the ranch for good. "Something is wrong with Belle. Okay? She's depressed, and she won't listen to me. So if you don't want me interfering, tell her to go to a doctor. She needs help."

Raleigh's stricken face seared itself into Marshall's mind. The dark circles under the eyes, the worry lines in his forehead—all told him what he should have seen before barging in. Raleigh was struggling as much as Belle was. And Marshall had no clue how to fix either of them.

He spun on his heel to leave.

"Marshall, wait."

He clenched his jaw but didn't move.

"You really think Belle's depressed?"

Did Raleigh sound hopeful? What an odd re-action. Who would be happy to find out their wife was depressed?

"Yeah, I do. Ainsley told me she thinks it's postpartum depression, but I didn't want to be-lieve it."

"That would explain a lot." He took off his hat and wiped his forehead. "I've been worried she's…"

"What?" Marshall narrowed his eyes, daring him to criticize his sister.

"Don't get mad." He thrust both palms out. "I thought maybe she didn't like being a mother. That she wouldn't ever take to it, if you get my drift."

"That's not the problem, Raleigh. I looked it up, and this depression thing is pretty common. But we should probably figure out how to get her to the doctor."

Raleigh nodded, exhaling loudly and looking at the floor.

Marshall turned. "I'm going to inspect fence for a while. By the way, I'm still going up to the house every afternoon, so don't ask me not to, and if you ever say it's because of Ainsley and not the babies, I'll knock you to the ground."

A grin spread across Raleigh's face. "What makes you think you can knock me down?"

He snorted. "Are we good?"

"Yeah. We're good."

Marshall headed back to the tack room and hoisted his saddle. That conversation hadn't gone as expected. Did Raleigh resent that he worked for him? The man definitely had a problem with his closeness with Belle, which was ridiculous. Belle was Marshall's twin, his only family. Didn't Raleigh get it?

And as for working here and helping with the babies…shouldn't Raleigh be thanking him instead of accusing him of flirting with Ainsley?

Marshall carried the saddle outside, his breath visible before him.

Maybe he'd made a big mistake quitting his job and moving here.

Well, so what if he had?

He didn't exactly have any alternatives.

It had been a terrific day! Ainsley wanted to spin in circles with her hands in the air and shout for joy. Instead she settled for knocking on Marshall's door that evening. When he opened it, she had to bite her lip to keep from swooning. He'd clearly just showered since his hair glistened with dampness. He wore a dark blue Henley pushed to his forearms, jeans and bare feet. She took a mental snapshot of the image to replay in her head later.

"Guess what?" She tore off her coat and slung it on a hook.

"What?"

"You know how your sister was holding Lila when you stopped by earlier? She helped me take care of the babies *all day*, and she didn't go to her room once!"

His mouth dropped open, and he blinked. "You're being serious?"

"I wouldn't kid about something this important."

He took her by the waist and pulled her into a quick hug. She almost gasped at his touch. Then he stepped back, his hand in his hair. "I can't believe it. That's great news."

"I know." She clapped her hands. "I offered to babysit tomorrow so she and Raleigh can get off the ranch for a while. I think they need to reconnect. Who knows, maybe a little shopping and a meal out will give them the boost they need."

"You offered to babysit so they can go on a date?" He sounded incredulous.

She nodded happily. "Mmm-hmm, and I told her not to hurry back. Your sister is actually really nice when she's not hiding in her room or insulting me."

Marshall was staring at her oddly. She ran her tongue over her teeth. Did she have lettuce stuck in her gums or something?

"Come on. We're getting out of here." He held up a finger. "First, let me get my socks." He raced to the bedroom and before she could figure out what he was doing, he was back.

"Getting out of here?" she asked. "What are you talking about?"

"You. Me. Sweet Dreams. We're going out."

"Why?"

"Because this is cause for celebration."

"O-kay." She scrunched her nose, looking down at her old lavender sweater. "I need to change first. I look terrible."

"No, you don't, you look incredible." He shoved his feet into shoes and unhooked both their coats.

"Wait, I at least need my purse." Had she been caught in a tornado? Everything was happening so fast.

She kind of liked it.

"Grab your purse. I'll start the truck. If you're not out there in fifteen seconds, I'm coming in after you." He gently pushed her out the door.

She laughed, enjoying the thought. "I'll meet you out here in a minute."

"Fifteen seconds."

She rolled her eyes. "Fine."

"Promise?"

She waved him off. Inside her cabin, she changed her sweater, ran a brush through her long hair and swiped on pink lip gloss before snatching her purse and locking the door behind her. She hopped into Marshall's truck. "What now?"

"Barbecue."

"Ooh, I like the sound of that."

"Me, too."

They drove in easy silence. Ainsley relaxed into the seat and let her thoughts scatter. She closed her eyes. Just for a moment…

"Ainsley?" A hand shook her arm. "Wake up. We're here."

She shivered, staring into Marshall's eyes. His tender expression jolted her awake.

"It's time to eat," he said.

She reached for her purse and got out of the truck. Marshall escorted her into the log building with a large hunter green sign spelling Roscoe's BBQ.

"It's your fault, you know." She gave him a sly glance as they stood inside the entrance.

"What is?" He told the hostess they needed a table for two. The teen gestured for them to follow her.

"Me falling asleep."

"Oh, yeah? You can't stop thinking about me or something?" His eyes teased her.

He had no idea how close he was to the truth, but she didn't want him knowing that.

"You wish." She playfully slapped his arm. "No, I noticed you've been heading over to the main house very early every morning."

He slid into the booth, deep grooves setting in his forehead.

"Yeah, well, not anymore," he said.

"What do you mean?" She sat across from him. Country music played over the speakers, and laughter erupted from nearby tables. The tangy scent of barbecue sauce made her stomach growl. "I hope you don't think I'm lecturing you. If you want to go over there and help, I'm not going to stop you."

"No, that's not it. Raleigh and I had a…disagreement earlier."

The way he paused at the word *disagreement* raised her suspicions.

"A disagreement, huh?" She leaned forward, giving him her full attention.

"He acts like he did me this big favor by letting me work on the ranch. I don't even want to work there. I could care less about cows and calves and riding out in the freezing cold constantly. If I had my way, I'd be back at Beatty

Brothers Repair, taking apart big machines every day."

She'd never seen him so riled up. She knew ranching wasn't his ideal job, but she hadn't realized how much he disliked it.

"Sorry, I didn't mean to pour all that on you." He rubbed his chin. "I guess his words hit me the wrong way."

"I get it." She propped her elbow on the table and rested her cheek on her hand. "You don't feel appreciated. And instead of him thanking you, he got defensive."

He nodded. "I don't even blame him, not really. He's the one getting up in the middle of the night with the babies, not Belle, the way I'd assumed. And I could be wrong, but I feel like dealing with the babies is way over his head, which brings out his prickly side."

The waitress stopped by and took their orders. Marshall's earlier good mood had changed to pensiveness, and Ainsley wanted to bring back his happy side.

"Tell me about your old job." She steered the conversation away from the ranch. She was going to enjoy this night. It was Friday, and they were at a hopping restaurant, and…she liked him. A lot.

"There's not much to tell."

"Sure there is. When did you learn how to repair big machinery? Tractors, right?"

"Yes, among other things." His eyes brightened. "One of the bonuses of living in the group foster home was that I found a part-time job after school as soon as I turned sixteen. I worked for an auto mechanic here in town. Jim Clark showed me basic auto repairs and maintenance, and I took to it naturally."

"I can tell you loved it." She couldn't take her gaze off his animated face.

"I did. Jim saw something in me and let me assist him more and more until I was doing repairs on my own. His brother had a ranch nearby, and his combine had broken down. I begged to go over there and have a look at it. I called the manufacturer, got the manual, talked to local ranchers known for fixing their own equipment, and I was hooked."

The waitress dropped off their drinks. After they thanked her, Ainsley unwrapped her straw. "So how did you end up in Cheyenne? Why didn't Belle move here when you guys turned eighteen?"

"Jim was retiring, and Belle already lived in the area. I didn't mind. I couldn't find a job in a repair shop right away, so I did some time at McDonald's. But I put applications in at every auto maintenance and repair shop, and within a few months, William Beatty hired me."

"Did you work there for long?"

"Ten years."

Ainsley took a long drink as she pondered what he'd said. Ten years at a job he loved. And he'd given it all up to move to Sweet Dreams. To work on a ranch so he could help his sister.

He was too good to be true.

Really, he was.

He tapped his knuckles on the table. "Maybe it's for the best Raleigh and I had it out."

"Why?"

"I told him to talk to Belle about seeing a doctor."

"How did he take it?"

"A lot better than I did. I still think he should push his schedule back an hour so he can feed the babies at five, though."

And just like that he was no longer too good to be true.

The words dropped to her stomach like a stone in a stream. Marshall had admitted Raleigh was already feeding the babies in the night. Belle could take the early-morning shift. Why did Marshall keep pampering his sister?

She gripped the glass. "Why don't you want Belle to do it?"

"If she's helping you during the day, she's going to be tired at night."

"Yes…but if she's not getting up with them, surely, she's getting enough sleep. And today was the first day she's helped me at all."

Marshall massaged the back of his neck. "So?"

"She's not made of crystal, Marshall. She won't shatter."

"You don't get it."

"I do get it. I think you're the one in denial."

He glowered. "Let's drop it."

"Fine with me." She looked around, and the festive atmosphere no longer felt joyful. She'd heard things like "you don't get it" and "drop it" many times over the years. Always when she confronted her father about his drinking.

Marshall isn't your father. Look at him. He's good and kind and generous.

Her dad had been good and kind and generous, too—when he was sober. But the drinking turned him into a different person. A blind man. Someone she couldn't rely on. Someone who didn't value himself the way she valued him.

Why did thinking about her father still hurt?

And why had he never reached out to her? She'd given him her number. Hadn't changed it. He could easily look up her address on the internet. But three years had passed without a word.

"Hey, Ainsley?"

She blinked away her turmoil and met Marshall's eyes. "Yes?"

"I'm sorry. Can we go back to celebrating?"

She gave him a smile. "Absolutely."

Maybe it wasn't right for her to compare Marshall to her dad. And maybe she was being too hard on him about Belle.

The hospital would be calling soon. A concrete job offer in her hand would go a long way to getting her thoughts back where they belonged.

She was a realist. Marshall had hammered it home to her ever since she'd met him that Belle came first in his life. Period.

Falling for him would be a disaster. Because she'd always come in second.

Chapter Eight

He'd messed things up with Ainsley. Late the next morning in the far pasture, Marshall injected a shot of medicine into a black calf. The animal was clearly sick, but the minute Marshall had started swinging the rope, the crafty gal had decided she wasn't ailing after all. Marshall had chased her for several minutes before catching an ankle and bringing her down. He murmured sweet nothings to her as he patted her side. The rest of the herd quietly grazed as if nothing was going on.

The cold air and clear skies gave him too much time to think. And his thoughts ping-ponged among Belle, the babies, Ainsley and Raleigh. Every time they bounced to Ainsley, he shooed them away. He'd disappointed her last night. He wasn't sure how or why, but he was 100 percent sure he had.

She'd been fine before he mentioned wanting Raleigh to take over the early-morning feeding. Why had she taken Raleigh's side, anyhow? She'd been so easy to talk to before that. Few people asked about his life, and she'd seemed genuinely interested.

What had he done wrong?

He prodded his horse into a trot to return to the stables. His chores were done for the day. Saturdays held a lighter workload for him. No doubt Raleigh wouldn't stop working until later in the afternoon. Let him be a glutton for punishment. The other cowboys were more than capable of handling the afternoon duties on their own.

After taking care of his horse, Marshall left the stables. He figured he'd clean up, then check on Ainsley and the babies. But after taking three steps, he halted, belatedly remembering Ainsley had offered to babysit the quadruplets so Belle and Raleigh could get away as a couple today.

But Raleigh was still out riding, which defeated the purpose.

One person did not a couple make.

Why was Ainsley so generous to his sister? Especially after giving so much energy to the children while Belle barely did a thing? While his sister had her good points, treating Ainsley nicely wasn't one of them. Yet Ainsley continued to shower her with kindness.

Shame shot an arrow into his heart.

If Ainsley could sacrifice for his sister, couldn't he sacrifice for Raleigh?

Forget it. I don't want to. I'm mad at him. He was a real jerk yesterday. He doesn't deserve my sacrifice.

He took four more steps toward the cabins. Stopped in his tracks. When he'd lived at Yearling Group Home, Dottie had made him and the other guys memorize scripture. One verse came to mind. "Blessed are the merciful: for they shall obtain mercy."

Ugh. He hated when his conscience reared up. He could practically hear Dottie's voice in his ear from all those years ago. "You can't earn salvation, hon. We all sin. And we show our thanks to Jesus by following His commands. Love God with all your heart, and love your neighbor as yourself."

He muttered, "Love your neighbor," and trudged back to the stables. Guess he was getting back in the saddle. To his surprise, Raleigh was already there brushing his horse.

"I was just coming to find you." Marshall gave him a hand.

"Oh, yeah? Why?"

"Ainsley offered to babysit so you and Belle

can go into Sweet Dreams and spend some time together."

"Belle mentioned it." Raleigh glanced up at him. "I'm worried about a section of fence out past the creek. I'm getting ready to drive my truck out there now."

Marshall clapped his hand on his shoulder. "Hey, man, why don't you let me handle the fence? Go home. Get cleaned up. Enjoy your wife. I'll help with the babies when I'm done, so you don't need to worry about hurrying back, okay?"

Raleigh slowly rose, blinking. "Really? You'd do that?"

"Sure."

He went through detailed instructions about the fence until Marshall finally laughed and said, "Enough. I've got this. Now get out of here."

Raleigh nodded, a smile tugging on the corner of his lips. "Thanks."

"You're welcome."

Watching his walk turn into a run lightened Marshall's heart. Offering to help had been the right thing to do. And fixing the fence wouldn't take more than an hour.

Then he could spend the rest of the day doing what he wanted—holding his nieces and nephews and spending time with Ainsley. If she wanted him around…

* * *

"He's not coming," Belle called from the hallway.

"It's still early." Ainsley made kissy faces at Max as she lifted him in front of her face. He licked his lips, his eyes growing wide. She brought him closer and kissed his tiny cheek. He smelled like baby shampoo. All the babies did—she'd given them baths earlier. She'd tried to get Belle involved, but to no avail. Belle had been curling her hair and picking out an outfit to wear. "Why don't you text him?"

Belle entered the living room wearing black leggings and a long, cream-colored sweater. Her hair lay in pretty curls over her shoulders, and her makeup highlighted her brown eyes and high cheekbones.

"You look gorgeous." Ainsley rose from the couch, holding Max to her chest. "I love your outfit."

"It's okay?" Belle held her arms out and turned back and forth. "It's not too tight? Oh, who am I kidding? It is. I'll never lose the baby weight."

"It's more than okay. It's perfect." Ainsley waved her concerns away. "And your curves look good on you. Send some of those my way, why don't you?"

Belle tugged on the sleeve of the sweater. "I

ordered this online a few weeks ago. It's so weird not knowing my size. I had to guess."

"Well, you guessed correctly." Ainsley set Max on the floor next to Ben, and she picked up Grace. "Why don't you relax for a while?"

Belle's eyes darted from the babies to the clock on the wall. It was after three. Then she dropped to sit on the couch. "I might as well. I've been stood up."

"He'll be here. He probably got tied up with the cows." Ainsley ran her fingers over Grace's head. The fine hair was soft. Ainsley would love to see her and Lila in matching headbands.

"The cows. Hmmph." Belle stretched her legs out on the couch and let her head fall back on the throw pillow. "Cattle is so much more important than anything going on in here." She waved her arm to take in the living room. "He hasn't even set up the Christmas tree."

"Do you get a real tree?" Ainsley sat on the other couch and made silly faces at Grace. The baby cooed in response.

"No, an artificial. Raleigh puts it together and strings the lights every year. He usually has it up by now. We like to wait until night falls, turn on Christmas music and decorate it together."

"Sounds wonderful." She glanced at Belle, who was chewing a fingernail. Maybe holding a baby would relax her. "Want to hold Lila?"

Belle turned her head away. "I'd better not."

Ainsley frowned. *What did that mean—she'd better not?* Sometimes the woman exasperated her. She snuggled Grace against her shoulder. The gurgles and aahs Grace uttered filled her heart. There was nothing better than holding a happy baby.

The sound of the back door opening made Belle sit up.

"Just let me get cleaned up, and we'll go." Raleigh tore through the living room on his way to the bedroom.

Thank You, Lord, for making him come through for her. Ainsley turned to Belle. "See? You two are going to have a great time. What are you going to do first?"

"I don't know." Belle's cheeks were flushed, and she stood, smoothing the sweater over her hips. "I haven't been to Lorraine's Mercantile in ages. She has such cute home decorations. Maybe I could find some frames. It would be nice to have the babies' pictures on the mantel."

"I agree." Ainsley made a game of opening and closing her mouth to entertain Grace.

"And I miss my peppermint mochas from The Beanery." Excitement infused her tone. "It's going to be so nice to get out for a while."

Ben let out a squawk.

"Is he okay?" Belle pivoted, looming over the activity mats. Her hand was over her chest.

"Why don't you check?" Ainsley said nonchalantly.

She peered down at him. "I think something's wrong."

Ainsley glanced at the boy. He stared up at the stuffed whale dangling above him. His face was growing red, and his feet pumped in irritation. "He's probably tired of being there. Pick him up and hold him."

Belle shot her a glance as if she was crazy, but she girded her shoulders and bent to pick him up. Sliding him out from under the activity bar, she reached under his armpits. "He's so light."

She was taken aback. *Of course he's light. He's a teeny-tiny baby.*

Belle placed him near her chest, patting his back. He quieted. "He's not crying."

"He likes being held."

Belle pressed her cheek to the top of his head for a moment. Ainsley admired the pair. Belle was striking, and the sight of her enjoying holding Ben brought a wonderful pressure to Ainsley's chest.

"You are a sight for sore eyes." Raleigh entered the room. He'd changed into a Western shirt and jeans. He crossed over to Belle and put his arms around her and the baby. "You're beautiful."

Ainsley looked away but not before seeing Belle's eyes glistening. Their love was obvious.

"And this little fella is sure handsome." Raleigh took Ben out of her arms and cradled him. He looked at Ainsley. "Where should I put him?"

"Let me set Grace down and I'll take him." Ainsley set her on the activity mat. Then she took Ben from Raleigh.

"Thank you, Ainsley," he said. "We appreciate this."

"You're welcome. Now get out of here and enjoy yourselves." She waved them away.

They laughed and headed out the front door. When Ainsley heard the truck rumble down the drive, she moved all the babies back into their bouncy seats, placed blankets over them and gave them pacifiers. She went to the kitchen and made herself a cup of coffee. By the time she returned, they'd all fallen asleep except for Lila, whose eyelids kept drooping. Ainsley switched the television on and clicked through to a Christmas movie.

Belle had seemed normal today. Well, as normal as Ainsley had seen her. She'd been easy to talk to and had actually picked up Ben. Usually Ainsley had to bring the babies to her. But Belle's comment about how light he was had been strange. Didn't Belle ever hold the babies when Ainsley wasn't around?

She'd feel better about the situation if Belle would see a doctor. Ainsley still believed she had postpartum depression. Maybe it was clearing up, though. Yesterday and today had been promising.

As the movie continued, she sipped the coffee and looked around the room. This house ranked a zero on the Christmas decoration scale. Belle had mentioned she wanted Raleigh to put up the tree. The man was likely exhausted. Ranching all day, up with the babies at night...it was no wonder he hadn't set up the Christmas tree.

She pulled a throw over her legs as she sprawled on the couch. She peered over to check the babies. Sleeping—except for Lila. The girl watched Ainsley as her binkie bobbed in rhythm. Ainsley swung her legs over and picked up the smallest of the quadruplets. She'd had special time with the other ones. Lila was so undemanding, Ainsley felt bad about giving her less attention than the other three.

"Not today, sweet one. You and I are going to hang out and watch the rest of *Home Alone*. What do you say to that?"

Lila looked up at her through sleepy eyes.

Ainsley lightly traced her finger across each of Lila's eyebrows, then her cheeks. Her eyelids closed, she let out a sigh of contentment and promptly fell asleep.

What would it be like to have a house like this to decorate for Christmas? A husband who would take her out on a date? A baby of her own to cuddle with on a cold Saturday in December?

She thought of Belle, who seemed to have it all, and drew her eyebrows together. Belle wasn't enjoying her blessings, but could Ainsley blame her? She had a real condition no one seemed to be concerned about. If Belle didn't continue to show improvement, Ainsley would have to talk to her. The guys could blow off Belle's behavior, but she couldn't. Not when it involved the children.

Maybe no one really had it all. The perfect life was an illusion. She wanted to believe finding happiness was possible, though.

The back door creaked. She craned her neck. Marshall came into view. He smiled when he saw her, and her breath caught in her throat.

He'd come over.

And he knew Belle wouldn't be around, which meant…he'd come over to be with her.

"I hope it's okay I'm here." Marshall glanced at Ben, Max and Grace all sound asleep in their bouncy seats. Then his heart hiccuped at the sight of Lila sleeping in Ainsley's arms. Ainsley—maternal, organized, generous—he hadn't realized a woman like her existed. With the throw spread over her legs, tendrils of blond hair escaping from her ponytail and her face flushed, she looked as appealing as a mug of hot cocoa. Better.

"Of course. I'm glad you came."

Phew. He'd been worried she was mad at him after arguing last night. At least she didn't hold a grudge.

"I told Raleigh I'd fix the fence, or I would have been here earlier." He took a seat in the chair kitty-corner from her. "What are you watching?"

"*Home Alone.* You missed all the good parts."

"I love that movie. I remember the first time I saw it. I couldn't believe their mansion and the decorations. I wanted to move right in."

She chuckled. "Same here." Her face full of love, she gazed down at Lila. "It was nice of you to help Raleigh out today. Belle was worried he wasn't coming, and when he arrived, she positively lit up."

"I'm glad. I didn't do it for Belle, though."

Questions lurked in her eyes.

"I thought of how you volunteered to take care of the babies, and your generosity touched me. I did it for Raleigh."

"Really?"

He sniffed, shrugging. "Well, for my sister,

too, I guess, but mostly because I knew it was the right thing to do."

Her eyes gleamed with appreciation, and he stared, unable to look away.

"What's the plan for tonight?" he asked.

"I don't have one. This was as far as I got."

"You're sure you don't mind me staying?"

"I'm sure," she said. "But you get all the stinky diapers."

"You got it." He settled deeper into the chair. "Did you get the gingerbread ornaments hung up? I want to see the end results."

She shook her head. "I haven't had time. I'm thinking I'll decorate my cabin tomorrow. I'll get the tree out. String the lights. Hang everything. You should stop by."

"Sounds…nice." He gulped. Did she really want him to come over? Or was she being polite? Maybe he'd been monopolizing her. Coming on too strong. She didn't have to spend every free minute with him, although he liked it when she did.

"You're still taking me to church, right?" she asked.

"Yes, church in the morning, and I'll come over after to help hang the ornaments."

The movie was almost over, and when it ended, Ainsley turned to him.

"I have an idea, but I want your opinion."

"Shoot." He tried to come up with what was on her mind but had no idea what this was about.

"Belle seemed down about not having the Christmas tree set up. And I know Raleigh is busy and tired, so…" Her face crinkled as her shoulders hiked upward. "Would you be willing to set up the tree tonight? We won't decorate it. We'll merely get it ready so they can."

"Sure. Why not?" He liked the idea. He took in the room full of baby stuff. The place needed some holiday cheer. "I think Raleigh keeps all the Christmas decorations in the garage attic."

"You're positive you don't mind?" She shifted Lila to her other arm.

"I think it's a great idea. In fact, I'll try to find the tree right now before the babies wake up." He stood, pointing to her. "And you can find another Christmas movie. We might as well get in the spirit, too."

She lifted the remote and winked. He laughed.

An hour later, he finished fluffing the artificial tree branches. He'd set it up in front of the picture window in the living room.

"Does it look okay?" he called.

Ainsley stood a few feet away, her finger under her chin and her eyes narrowed. "Can you move it an inch or two to the left?"

He moved it. "Better?"

"Yes. Right there. How are you at stringing lights?"

"Terrible." He had no problem admitting it.

"I'll help."

"Good."

She dug through the plastic bins and found boxes of white lights and an extension cord. "Give me a sec to unravel these."

"You got it." He padded over to the babies, all still sleeping. They'd be waking up soon, and then he and Ainsley would be busy warming bottles and changing diapers. "We'd better hurry."

She laughed, holding up a tangle of lights. He took one end from her hands, trying not to breathe in her perfume, but it hit him anyway.

What was he doing? The woman looked good, smelled amazing and was nicer than anyone he'd ever met. He was falling for her, and not gently like a feather drifting to the ground. This was more like a brick hitting pavement. Hard.

"You're into Christmas, aren't you?" he asked. Maybe she'd start talking and he'd forget about her perfume.

"I love it. The most wonderful time of the year." She grinned and started weaving the strand around the bottom of the tree. She bumped into him, and he backed up so she could keep going around.

"What was your best Christmas?" He watched her placing the lights here and there.

"Easy. My thirteenth."

"Tell me about it."

Her face fell.

Why would she be down about her best Christmas? Something wasn't adding up.

"Dad and I were living near the border of Montana. He was the night hand for a cattle ranch. He'd been doing well there, better than at the previous ranch, anyway. One day we went into town, and he asked me what I wanted for Christmas. My winter coat was too small, and the elbows were worn, so I told him I wanted a new winter coat. As we walked through town on our way to the clothing store, I remember pressing my nose to the jeweler's. There was a heart-shaped necklace in the window, and in the center was my birthstone. Tiny diamonds surrounded it. It was the prettiest thing I'd ever seen."

"What's your birthstone?" He could picture her as a young girl with big eyes for a necklace.

"Aquamarine." She motioned for him to give her the next strand. "I must have drooled a little too much, because Dad noticed. He asked me if I liked it, but I couldn't bring myself to say yes.

Money was always in short supply, and I really needed a coat."

"I can relate to that," he said. "Having clothes that fit was an issue for me most of my life, too. So what happened?"

"We found a new coat on clearance, and I was relieved, but part of me couldn't stop thinking about the necklace. On Christmas morning, I ran out to our little tree in the living room of our cabin. Dad was smiling, and he held out a small paper bag. It was the necklace."

She paused, the lights dangling from her hands, and stared dreamily at the tree.

The story choked him up in a good way. He was glad she had nice memories.

She sighed, but rather than adding to the joy of the moment, it sounded sad.

"He went out that night. Didn't come home until the next afternoon. When I was in the shower, he snuck into my room and stole the necklace. Then he left again. I looked everywhere for it until it hit me he'd taken it. I didn't want to be right, but I was. He'd hocked it. It broke my heart, Marshall. My dad could be the best and the worst, the same as my thirteenth Christmas was."

He took the lights out of her hands and drew her into his arms. Rested his chin on the top of her head. Her soft hair teased his neck. He wanted to take away the bad memories. Confront her father and smack him upside the head. He wanted…

"I'm sorry, Ainsley. I wish no one had ever let you down, especially your dad."

She took two steps back, ducking her chin. "I learned to rely on myself."

"You don't have to do it all alone, though."

Her laugh sounded brittle. "I guess you don't know me at all. *Alone* is my middle name."

He frowned. How was he supposed to reply to that? He couldn't. In many ways his middle name was the same. Well, that wasn't true. He had Belle. He'd always had Belle, even when they weren't together.

"I think your middle name should be changed." He looked into her eyes. "To *generous. Special.*"

She blinked up at him. "I think I'd better stick with *alone.*"

He stepped back, unexpectedly hurt by her words. He could take a hint. If she wanted to be alone, he'd honor her wishes, even if it went against everything he felt for her. They didn't have a future together. He knew it. She knew it. And he'd better get it through his thick skull before he did something stupid like fall in love with her.

Chapter Nine

Ainsley's arm brushed Marshall's as she reached for the hymnal the next morning. A skittering sensation rippled over her skin. She scooted an inch away. There was no sense in being closer to the man than necessary. And if an innocent touch was affecting her this much, she'd be smart to move even farther away. She didn't, though. Flipping through the book, she passed the hymn and carefully backtracked, peeking over at Marshall. He wore a button-down shirt with jeans and cowboy boots. If she had to pick the ideal guy to attend church with, Marshall fit the criteria. He was different from the men she'd known. Different from her father.

Marshall was reliable. Trustworthy.

The piano plucked out a spirited tune, and she focused on the words of the first verse. But her mind wandered to the past. To the days when she'd believed her dad was invincible. He'd been her hero. He'd let her down plenty as a child, but he'd also found ways to come through for her, no matter how small. She'd loved him so much.

As the congregation began to sing, her chest grew tight. She didn't attempt to sing along. The past was determined to consume her mind today.

When had her father gotten worse with his drinking? By the time she'd turned eight, for sure. Maybe she'd noticed it more, or his circumstances could have been harder. Regardless, things had changed. His weekend binges turned into nightly disappearances. Her mother lost every morsel of joy—her mouth had thinned to a permanent tight line.

Ainsley had known her dad had a problem with alcohol. When he was home and drinking, he turned into a different person. An angry person who frightened her or a sobbing mess she pitied. The guys her father worked with all thought he was great—a stand-up guy who drank too much at times.

After her mother left, Ainsley had been his keeper. She'd lived with constant anxiety, little sleep and the daily fear he would drive home drunk and either kill someone or die himself. She never had friends over. She really hadn't had friends at all. She'd constantly been hiding his problem.

She'd always thought if she could get rid of all the alcohol—if she could get him to stop drinking—everything would be all right. She'd get him clean. Save him from himself.

What a laugh that had been.

She'd helped him get sober more than once. He'd always gone back to drinking.

The day she'd finally left had been excruciating. For most of her life she'd been convinced he would die if she wasn't around. The minute she'd driven away, the dam of emotion she'd repressed most of her childhood had gushed out, and it had taken months to get to a point where she didn't worry about him every minute.

She still worried about him at times.

For the past couple of years, she'd slept peacefully, no longer worried about how to pay the bills, protect herself from his angry words or question if she'd done a good enough job hiding the few things she valued. The late-night stumbling, rage and the uncontrollable sobbing of a nearly broken man were things of the past. She no longer tiptoed around trying to prevent her father from destroying himself.

It wasn't that she didn't care. She did. She still cared.

She just couldn't fix him.

And she could freely admit she'd been addicted to saving her dad the same way he was addicted to the bottle.

Her eyes welled up, and she shut the hymnal and sat back, forcing her lungs to take deep breaths. Why was she thinking about this now, anyhow? She'd dealt with it. Moved on. She didn't need to cry about him.

Lord, why is this coming up again? I've worked through it. I know I'm not Dad's keeper. I have no intention of slipping back into that role. Please take this burden from me. I can't go back to being full of anxiety all the time.

The pastor said the final prayer, and Ainsley whispered, "Amen." She hoped Marshall didn't want to discuss the sermon on the way home, because she hadn't focused on a single word. And she really didn't want to share what had been on her mind in its place.

After an usher excused them, they joined the crowd and ran into Marshall's friends at the coat rack.

"We're all going over to the diner for breakfast," Amy said as she helped Ruby into her winter coat. Ainsley had to stop herself from staring at the dear little girl. Amy continued. "Why don't you and Marshall join us?"

"I'll have to check with him." Ainsley turned to Ruby. "Are you getting excited for Christmas?"

Ruby stared up at her through big sparkly

eyes and nodded. She clutched Amy's hand. "Mommy and I are baking cookies later. I get to help frost them."

Amy smoothed her hand over Ruby's hair. "She's a very good froster. Ruby knows her sprinkles."

Ainsley chuckled. "You can never have too many sprinkles."

"We got a new kitty cookie cutter. I have a kitty named Fluffy, and she is fat." Ruby opened her hands to show how big the cat was.

"I love kitties. Especially big fluffy ones." Ainsley walked with them toward the door. Behind her, Marshall talked to Nash and Clint.

"How are the quadruplets?" Lexi, Clint's wife, asked, squeezing by the men. "I've been meaning to stop by, but I wasn't sure if Belle would mind or not. I'm sure her hands are full."

Amy bit her lower lip. "And I should bring over another casserole. I'm sure they're running out at this point. I'd love a chance to see those babies."

"How many babies are there?" Ruby asked, her eyes wide. An older gentleman opened the door, and they filed outside into the cold air.

"Four," Ainsley replied. "And they're the sweetest things. So adorable."

"Excuse me." Marshall tugged on Ainsley's sleeve. She turned as a gust of wind blasted her.

His brown eyes gleamed. "Would you be okay with getting breakfast with my friends at Dottie's right now? If you need to get back, it's no problem."

"I'd love to get breakfast."

Amy and Lexi exchanged big smiles.

"Good," Lexi said. "You can tell us all about the babies over hotcakes."

"We're both kind of obsessed with infants right now." Amy held Ruby's hand as they started down the porch steps. Nash was at Amy's side in a heartbeat, taking her by the elbow. Clint held Lexi's hand. Which left Ainsley next to Marshall.

The comments about the babies and the attention of their husbands made Ainsley wonder. Lexi and Amy must be trying to get pregnant.

She watched them joking and laughing on their way to the parking lot and fought back envy. She tried not to want more than she already had, but it was impossible to deny the lure of deep friendships, church on Sundays together, a doting husband, the chance to have a family.

Besides Tara, Ainsley didn't have any close friends. What would it be like to have a whole group of people to spend time with on a regular basis?

Marshall helped her into the passenger seat of his truck. "Are you okay?"

"Yes." She nodded, her brittle smile frozen in place.

"Sure something isn't bothering you?" He climbed up, shut his door and started the engine.

"I'm not used to…" She almost blurted out the truth. That she'd avoided developing friendships for most of her life. Her dad's behavior when he drank had embarrassed her, and since he'd always been drinking… She thought about the Al-Anon meetings she'd attended. She had nothing to be ashamed of. She could tell Marshall the truth. "I'm not great at this sort of thing."

"What sort of thing?" He turned onto the road.

"Friends." She wrung her hands in her lap. "When I was younger, I always tried to hide the reality of my father's alcoholism from people, and I haven't had a lot of friends because of it."

As trees and countryside sped by, he glanced her way. "I know what you mean, and Clint and Nash do, too, so don't worry about them. Clint has no parents. He got bounced around to various foster homes before we met. And Nash's mom was a drug addict. His life was pretty rough. My friend Wade had a less-than-stellar childhood, too."

Hearing it made her feel a little better, but… those were *his* friends. "What about Lexi and Amy?"

"I think they had normal families." He

shrugged. "But they never thought less of Clint or Nash, so I can't imagine they'd think less of you."

Maybe not, but she couldn't shake the feeling she was damaged goods. If they knew how she'd left her father, would they judge her for it?

"We're just having breakfast, Ainsley. They don't need to know your life story. They're good people. You have nothing to worry about. I mean, would you think differently of them if they had rough childhoods?"

"No." She stared at the line of parked cars in front of the diner. Of course she wouldn't think less of them.

Why was she even worried? It didn't matter if they accepted her or not. She was leaving in a few weeks. A life in Sweet Dreams wasn't on her agenda, and therefore making lasting friendships with Lexi and Amy wasn't going to happen.

If she could choose the ideal town to live in, Sweet Dreams would be it. Ainsley had already bonded with Lexi and Amy, and they'd been chatting for only an hour. She sipped her third cup of coffee and colored a flower on a place mat with Ruby as Lexi and Amy filled her in on their holiday plans. She'd eaten way too many pancakes, but she didn't care. They'd been delicious.

The more she talked to the ladies, the more

she believed they'd already accepted her and nothing in her past would change their opinions of her.

It was a heady thought.

"It's too bad you're leaving after New Year's." Lexi sighed, lifting her mug for another drink. "We can never convince Marshall to leave the ranch. But with you here—I mean, he's been to church, and we're all having breakfast together—that's saying something."

"Oh, you're mistaken." Ainsley waved dismissively. "He's here because we both need a break from the reality of quadruplets."

"I hope Belle and Raleigh bring them to church soon." Amy spread jelly on a slice of toast. "I can't wait to see the sweethearts out and about."

Ainsley frowned, selecting a blue crayon to fill in her flower. She hadn't thought about it, but Belle and Raleigh hadn't taken the babies out at all. Shouldn't they have a well-child visit soon?

"I like your flower." Ruby looked up at her. "Can you tell the babies' mommy to bring them to church next week? I want to see them, too."

"Well, I can try, Ruby." She tried to reassure the girl, but she didn't foresee Belle bringing the babies to church so soon. "It's not easy getting four infants bundled up and in their car seats, though."

"What if she brought two? Just the girls." Ruby drew a sun in the corner of the place mat. "The boys can stay home."

Amy tucked her lips under and looked at the ceiling, clearly mortified.

"Do you have a picture of them?" Ruby set her crayon on the table. "Mommy, do you have any stickers?"

"Let me see…" Amy rummaged through her purse.

A picture… Ainsley thought back to her and Belle's conversation about buying picture frames for the quadruplets.

"Lexi?" Ainsley asked. "You're a wedding planner, so you must know local photographers. Do you know anyone who might be willing to come out to Dushane Ranch and take Christmas pictures of the quadruplets? I think Belle would love some professional photos."

"Oh, great idea!" Lexi grinned.

"I know that tone." Sitting next to her, Clint frowned. "What's going on over here?"

"Ainsley suggested hiring a local photographer to take pictures of all the babies. Isn't it a fabulous plan?"

He had the deer-caught-in-headlights look. "Um, yeah. I guess."

"I'll tell you what, ladies. I'll bring my phone

over and snap the pics myself." Nash wriggled his eyebrows. "Save them some money."

"I can't believe you even suggested that." Amy shook her head and playfully slapped his arm.

"What? I can take pictures as good as the next guy." His tone was all teasing.

"If you mean taking blurry photos or ones with your thumb in the picture, then yes, I agree."

"You wound me, Amy." He clasped his heart.

She rolled her eyes, a smile teasing her lips.

"I'll see if Marjory or Russell can come out," Lexi said to Ainsley. "Here's my cell number. Let me know a good time to come over. Do you think Belle would mind if Amy and I came over, too?"

"That's not my place to say." At their crestfallen faces, she lifted her hands. "But I can ask."

They both brightened.

Marshall leaned in next to Ainsley so only she could hear. "You come up with the best ideas, you know."

Her cheeks felt hot. Or maybe it was just his warm breath so close to her. She tucked the compliment away. "Well, I want the babies' first Christmas to be special. For everyone."

"I hate to break up the party, but we have to skedaddle," Nash announced. Ruby slipped between the tightly packed chairs and hopped onto his lap. "Did you get filled up, RuRu?"

"Miss Dottie gave me extra whipped cream." She patted her tummy.

"I might have to have a talk with her." He pretended to be stern.

"No, Daddy, I like the whipped cream!"

"But she didn't give *me* any extra." He stood, lifting her to his hip.

"I'll tell her to give you some, too." She wound her arms around his neck, hugging him.

Ainsley hung back as everyone said goodbye and filed outside. Lexi and Amy gave her quick hugs. In her daddy's arms, Ruby waved. The moment seemed to suspend in time, and Ainsley watched each of them pair off, certain she'd been given one of the loveliest gifts she'd ever receive.

She'd been one of them for a morning. Part of their circle of friends.

Marshall lit the kindling under the logs in Ainsley's fireplace that afternoon. As flames rose and caught the wood, he relaxed. Being here felt better than familiar. It felt like home.

The scent of cinnamon and cloves reached him as he watched snow falling outside. He'd enjoyed breakfast with his friends earlier, and it had opened his eyes to something he hadn't realized. He missed them. They'd found wives, and he was alone. Hanging out with them some-times felt uncomfortable because they had part-ners and he didn't.

He'd also been surprised when Ainsley admit-ted she worried the women wouldn't like her. As if anyone wouldn't like her. It wasn't possible.

Earlier, church had raised some weird ques-tions inside him, like what was he doing with his life? Did he see himself working on Dushane Ranch forever?

He'd gotten the most pressing urge to pray about his path, which made no sense. He already had his priorities straight. Family came first. But he'd said a short prayer anyhow.

"I'll be right out." Her melodious voice bright-ened the room.

He walked over to the small fake Christmas tree she'd set up on an end table near the front window. White lights twinkled happily from it. Made him think of his own undecorated cabin next door. Maybe he would hang a wreath or buy a few candles in town. Snazzing up his place for the holidays wouldn't kill him. Or maybe he'd just keep coming over here.

Ainsley had a bounce in her step as she came out of the bedroom. "I've finished tying the rib-bons. All that's left is to hang them."

"Tell me where they go."

"Oh, anywhere. Just start putting them on the

tree." She waved him over to the kitchen table, where she'd lined up the cookies they'd baked and decorated last week. Each had a white ribbon tied in a loop.

He selected two ornaments. They smelled delicious. If they weren't going on the tree, he'd be tempted to eat them. "That was nice of you to suggest having the babies' pictures taken. Do you want me to talk to Belle about it?"

"I'll do it. I don't mind." Her glowing face made his stomach flip-flop. "I think she'll be excited."

"The photographer will come here, right?" He went to the tree and placed a gingerbread star on one of the upper branches. It slipped, but he caught it before it fell to the floor. "That was a close one."

"Lexi made it sound as if a photographer would come here. Raleigh and Belle haven't gotten the babies out of the house yet that I know of. I hope they have doctor's appointments set up for the children. It's important to find out if they're all gaining enough weight."

"I don't know anything about that." He scratched his neck. "Honestly, I can't imagine taking all four of those babies into town."

"They're going to have to get them out at some point."

"True." It was another conversation he didn't

want to have with his sister. She was just starting to make progress taking care of the babies on the ranch. He didn't want to stress her out by making her think about going into town with them.

Ainsley held up a gingerbread boy. "I'll mention it when I ask her about the photo session."

Her take-charge personality was such a relief.

"Hey, no more baby talk." Marshall wagged his finger. "This is our day off, remember?"

She gave him a sheepish smile. "Okay. I know what we need." She found a playlist on her phone. Soft instrumental Christmas music began to fill the room. Marshall wasn't sentimental, but, in an environment like this, he could become downright sappy.

"I'm sure Christmas is different for you this year considering you were in Cheyenne previously. How do you usually celebrate?" Ainsley hung an ornament on one of the branches.

"It is different. Plus, this Christmas is a first for all of us now that the babies arrived. I used to drive here for Christmas Eve and Christmas Day. It was nice. We'd go to church and open presents and have a good steak dinner."

She brushed past him on her way to hang an ornament. He held his breath at her light touch.

"I'm guessing none of that will change." She tilted her head to watch him. "Except you might have cattle to feed this year."

He tried not to grimace, but he knew he wasn't fooling Ainsley into thinking he loved working on the ranch. He'd made his choice, though, so he'd make the best of it.

"Yeah, if Raleigh has anything to say about it, I'll probably be checking miles of fence come Christmas morning." He put another ornament up. "You know, the first year Belle and I lived together after high school was the best. We didn't have any money, but we had a lot of fun. We got gag gifts from the dollar store and wrapped them up. Neither of us had a clue how to cook, but she decided she was going to make a recipe from some fancy cookbook. The meal wasn't bad, but, let's just say she's much better in the kitchen now."

"And you're a fantastic cook. When did you learn how?" Ainsley shifted her weight to one hip, not seeming to care if an ornament dangled from her finger.

"I've had a lot of time on my hands in the past couple of years. I messed around with some easy recipes. Found that I liked it. And, to be honest, Clint was always making good food. I figured if he could cook, then I could, too."

"Do you always copy your friends?" Her green-gold eyes glinted with humor.

"Whenever they do something smart." His gaze met hers. Something simmered between them. Something good. And terrifying. He found himself wanting to take her by the hand, tug her to him and...

"They seem like great guys." She broke eye contact, and disappointment hit him like a punch in the chest. He should have extended the moment, reached over. Instead, he cleared his throat.

"They are. They're the best friends a guy could have."

"Family men." She nodded, hanging the ornament. "Do you see yourself copying that, too?"

A gingerbread house swung slightly from his finger. He'd never contemplated copying them on getting a wife and family, but if it was with someone like Ainsley, he'd be tempted.

You fool, there is no one like Ainsley. She stood before him—unique, incredible.

And she was leaving soon. While he would stay.

Because Belle needed him. She would always need him.

He walked back to the table, oddly disappointed. From the minute he'd been born, he'd never had a chance at a normal life. And he didn't see himself having one now.

What was normal anyhow?

He stayed silent, allowing a vision of a different way of filling his days to flit through his mind. Repairing big machines. Near Ainsley.

It all sounded like gumdrops and Christmas cheer—a bunch of made-up nonsense for a television movie. Sure, Belle and Raleigh were okay right now. But what would happen if things grew more strained between them? Or if something happened to one of the babies?

Marshall couldn't make any woman, including Ainsley, promises of forever he couldn't and wouldn't keep.

"I take it you don't want a family?" Ainsley had crept up behind him.

"My life is here."

Disappointment slid down her face. He felt like a jerk, knew she felt the connection between them, too. But honesty was the best policy. He wasn't one of those guys who flirted and broke a girl's heart.

The only heart getting broken would be his.

Chapter Ten

Ainsley had to do a better job at distancing herself emotionally from the babies…and from Marshall. Time was running short. She'd be gone, and they'd be here, and she wouldn't be spending her evenings eating dinner with Marshall anymore. Maybe scolding herself for the seventy-fifth time would make it sink in. She'd programmed the thought on auto-play days ago, and it still hadn't gotten through.

Here it was, almost five on Thursday, and Grace and Ben were as cranky as could be. Ainsley held one in each arm and bounced them. She hoped they would be happy tomorrow when the photographer arrived. Belle had seemed excited about the idea of having their photos taken when Ainsley asked her about it on Monday. And Ainsley had been relieved to find out the babies were scheduled to see the doctor after Christmas.

Ben let out a squawk.

She ground her teeth as she glanced at the Christmas tree in the front window. It still wasn't decorated. She and Marshall had set the boxes of ornaments next to it after getting it ready last weekend. Why hadn't Raleigh and Belle decorated it? It wouldn't take more than an hour to get the bulbs up.

Grace let out a cry, and Ainsley strolled around the room, gently bouncing the babies as she went.

Everything about that undecorated tree annoyed her right now.

Actually, life in general irritated her.

Her cell phone rang.

What now? She let out a long-suffering sigh. She could call to Belle, but the swish-swish of the treadmill told her it would be futile. The woman had been working out all week—more than once a day. At first, Ainsley had thought it was a step in the right direction. But she'd soon realized it had become a new excuse to avoid dealing with the children.

She made her way to the end table and checked the phone. Didn't recognize the number.

Her weary body yelled to ignore it, but…what

if it was her father? She'd kept the same cell phone number all these years on the off chance he'd finally call her.

Hope mingled with dread.

The holidays had always seemed to make him worse. What if it was someone telling her that her lifelong fear had come true—her dad had drank himself to death? She could barely stand the thought.

She had to answer it.

After setting Grace and Ben on a baby blanket on the floor, she answered the phone. "Hello?"

Both infants started crying loudly. Frantically, she looked around for their pacifiers while trying to shush them.

"Ainsley Draper? This is Beth Leopald from Ivinson Memorial Hospital."

Her heart stopped beating momentarily, then it tripped over itself it was beating so fast. The hospital! The job!

"Hi, it's great to hear from you." She found the pacifiers and gave one to each baby. Thankfully, they quieted down.

Beth continued. "We've made a decision, and we're offering you the position. Are you still available to begin the first week of January?"

She'd gotten the job!

"Yes, I am available."

"Good. I'll give Peg Denton your number to set up a training schedule. As for your salary…"

They discussed the job particulars for several minutes before ending the call. Then she let out a whoop.

The swish-swish slowed, and Belle appeared, toweling off her neck. "What's going on?"

"I got the job at the hospital!" Ainsley lifted her hands. "Aaah!"

The color drained from Belle's face.

"Belle?" Ainsley crossed over to her. "Are you okay? Come. Sit down." She led her to the couch and urged her to sit.

"I guess this means you'll be leaving."

Ainsley bristled at her accusing tone. Wasn't she happy for her?

"Not until the end of the month."

Belle stood abruptly and began to pace. Her color returned. "Well, now that I'm exercising, I'll be fine with the babies."

"If you're concerned, why don't you stay out here with us now? It will help you get adjusted."

"I don't need to get adjusted," she snapped. "I know how to do this."

"Then why don't you?" She hadn't meant to say it, but maybe it needed to be asked.

"Because…"

Ainsley waited, hoping Belle would say something that made sense, that explained her baffling behavior in terms that didn't scream postpartum depression.

"Because we pay you to do it." She stuck her nose in the air.

Really? She wanted to shout in frustration. Instead, she counted to three. "I think you should consider seeing a doctor."

"And I think you should mind your own business."

"A lot of new mothers deal with postpartum depression."

"I'm not depressed."

"It's especially common for mothers of multiples. A doctor could help. There are medications—"

Belle huffed. "Is that what you want? Me to be drugged up?"

"Of course not! I want you to enjoy your babies."

"Well, I already do, so let's drop it."

Ainsley clenched her jaw. "Fine."

"Fine." Belle narrowed her eyes. "The baby outfits for the photo shoot arrived. Have them ready tomorrow by four thirty." Then she sailed out of the room. Two beeps and the swish-swish of the treadmill met Ainsley's ears.

Wow. Had Belle really just gone there?

She should quit. Walk into that woman's room and tell her off.

Ainsley looked down at four innocent faces. They'd captured her heart. Ben, Max, Lila and Grace meant more to her than she wanted to admit.

She'd make it through the holidays, drive back to Laramie and never look back.

Well, maybe she'd look back now and then. She cared too much about the quadruplets to ever forget them.

And Marshall?

She doubted she had it in her to forget him. She wasn't sure she even wanted to. But from now on, she couldn't linger at his place after dinner. She'd been getting too close to him. The job in Laramie was hers. Her life wasn't here, and Marshall's was. The sooner she made peace with it, the better.

In the summer, he tolerated ranch work, but in the winter? He could take the cold for only so long before dreading the job. Today had been particularly cold and miserable. Last year at this time, he'd been protected from the wind in a pole barn in southern Wyoming. He could still feel the grease from the engine parts as he'd puzzled over why the tractor wouldn't run. The week before he'd worked on a drill rig, which had been fun. He'd been fascinated by all the moving parts. Now the only thing he looked forward to was his dinners with Ainsley. In Cheyenne after Belle had left, he'd dreaded evenings, but living here, they'd become his favorite time of the day.

As he strode through the barn, he couldn't help growing nostalgic for the smell of tools and oil and metal. The stench of manure had never measured up.

When he emerged into the fresh air, he broke into a jog. Dusk was falling, and he'd put chicken and noodles in the slow cooker this morning. Every afternoon he stopped at the main house for an hour to help with the babies, but he looked forward to his relaxing dinners with Ainsley more than the time with the quads.

Like chocolate syrup on vanilla ice cream, she made life richer, sweeter.

After letting himself into his cabin, he took a short hot shower and changed into jeans and a gray sweatshirt. He heard her knock as he ran a comb through his wet hair.

He opened the door and let her in. She had a radiance about her, like she'd been dipped in happy powder.

"Guess what?" She practically tore off her coat.

"What?"

"The hospital called and offered me the job!"

Disappointment fell to his toes faster than a lug wrench slipping from his grasp.

"That's great." He forced a smile on his face, but he doubted he was fooling her with it. He'd known she was leaving. She was never meant to stay. So why did it hurt so much hearing it confirmed?

"This is going to give me the boost I need to be accepted into nursing school this year. I can feel it."

He could picture her smiling at patients in her scrubs, and a wave of jealousy hit him so hard he was surprised he didn't fall over.

"You'll get in." He turned away, not wanting her to see what was likely written all over his face. He cared about her. Wanted her to stay. Couldn't imagine what life here would be like without her around. Moving to the kitchen, he distracted himself with dinner. He turned off the slow cooker and brought the chicken and noodles to the table.

Ainsley began putting the silverware down. "By the way, Belle and I had an argument earlier. I think it's only fair to warn you I told her to see a doctor about postpartum depression."

A stabbing pain shot through his chest, and his pulse raced. The postpartum depression subject had not been received well when he'd mentioned it a few weeks ago. He could imagine how Belle took it this time.

"For the record, she told me to mind my own business." Ainsley took a seat and folded her hands on the table. "Also, she's been exercising all week."

"That's good." He joined her, but from her tone, the exercise thing didn't sound positive.

"Normally I would agree with you, but in this case, I don't think it's helping. She's merely using it to avoid taking care of the children."

Too many things were coming at him at once. He ladled out food for each of them.

"Exercising has to be better than sleeping all the time." He folded his hands and waited for Ainsley to pray over the meal. When she'd finished, she poked her spoon around the bowl.

"It's not, Marshall." Her pretty eyes filled with empathy. "We've got to get her on board with the babies soon, and I don't know how it will happen if no one will admit the obvious. Belle needs to see a doctor."

His spoon slipped from his fingers to the table, and he leaned back, wiping his stubble with his hand. He wanted her to stop talking. Or to at least stop badgering him about Belle and the doctor. His sister wouldn't listen. And he couldn't make her.

"I know you don't want to hear this—" her

voice was low, quiet "—but with Christmas around the corner and me leaving soon after that…the sooner she gets help, the better."

He didn't know what to say. Belle wasn't going to agree to see the doctor. He had no solution up his sleeve.

"Just think about it." She took a bite of her food. "Mmm…this is delicious. You've outdone yourself."

"Thanks." He'd lost his appetite. And the more he thought about it, the more he resented being put on the spot about his sister. "She's getting better, you know."

She blinked, then captured his gaze. "Is she? How can you tell?"

"She…" He thought back on the past weeks. "It's in the facts. I don't go over there at night anymore. She and Raleigh are getting along better. The babies don't cry all day. You and I don't help on Sundays."

Ainsley tucked her lips under, avoiding eye contact.

"We've just transferred the baby care, spread it around," she said. "Raleigh is on night duty. I take care of them all day. Your sister is not better. She simply has more help now."

"And she should have more help. Especially if what you're saying is true." He slid his finger under his collar. His cabin had gone from warm to blazing.

"I'm not saying this to make you mad or to get into a fight." She sat straighter, setting her spoon down.

"Then why are you saying it?" He hated how harsh he sounded, but he couldn't help it.

Her eyes widened as if she'd had a lightbulb moment. He dreaded whatever she was about to say.

"I'm not your mother, Marshall. You can trust me. You couldn't trust her because she ignored the truth and made you pay the price. She put Belle in danger. But I'm trying to protect your sister. Don't be like your mother and ignore reality because it's more convenient. I think we both know if Belle doesn't get help, you'll be the one raising the children after I leave. That's a high price to pay."

Each word hit him in the gut. Was she comparing him to his mother? *No. No way.* And to suggest he didn't care about his sister? He crumpled his napkin and threw it on the table.

"That's the difference between you and me. I don't put a price on raising children." He regretted the words instantly. Her stricken face made him regret them even more. Why would he say that? What was wrong with him?

She pushed away from the table and stood.

"Did you ever stop and think maybe I meant it was a high price for Belle to pay? She's their mother. She wanted those babies. And if she doesn't start taking care of them, she won't be close to her own flesh and blood."

With that, she crossed to the hall, put her boots on, unhooked her coat and walked out the door.

The click of the latch froze him in place. All he could do was stare ahead.

He was not ignoring reality.

He got up, almost knocking over the chair as he did. His sister was fine. They'd had a weak, delusional mother. Belle probably didn't even know how to be a parent. Ainsley was wrong. Yeah, he'd have to help Belle out more after Ainsley left, but big deal. That's what family did. They helped each other.

"Don't ignore reality..."

He braced his hands against the kitchen counter. He had Belle's best interests in mind. Always had. He'd sacrificed for her before, and he would again. If Ainsley didn't understand it, well...

Maybe it was best for all of them she would be leaving soon.

Why did she even bother trying to help?

Ainsley stalked back and forth in front of her muted television later that night. She'd called Tara after leaving Marshall's, and Tara had agreed with her. Marshall, Raleigh and Belle were living in a fantasy world, one that would come crashing down sooner rather than later. Ainsley didn't want to be here when it did.

But she didn't want to leave either.

Marshall's words had cut right to the marrow. Didn't he have any idea how much she wanted a family of her own? She thought of Belle, who at this moment could be cherishing her babies but was probably power walking on the treadmill. Or Raleigh, out prowling the pastures when his offspring could use a cuddle. Marshall was no better. He acted like he was Mr. Caring, but was it really caring to watch a loved one fall into an abyss and miss out on the best things in life?

Hardly.

She sat back on the couch and clutched a throw pillow to her stomach. Belle treated her like the hired help—which she was—but she didn't appreciate the condescension. And Marshall accused her of taking care of the babies only for the money.

Emotion pressed against the backs of her eyes. Didn't he notice she'd gone above and beyond her duties to help Belle get engaged with her children? And what about the ways she'd tried to help—babysitting and setting up the Christmas tree and lining up tomorrow's photo shoot?

No one appreciated her.

She'd done so much for them. She cared about them. She wanted the babies to have a wonderful life.

Squeezing her eyes shut, she willed away the tears. This wasn't worth it. Being the baby nurse for the Dushanes had always been a temporary gig.

Why did she feel the need to save every hurting thing that landed in her path? They never wanted her help—not her father, not Belle, not Marshall. So why did she keep putting herself out there? Why did she want to help people who refused to take responsibility for their actions?

She tossed the pillow to the side. At least Marshall had shown his true feelings tonight. She'd been growing too close to him. All the times taking care of the babies together, dinners, church services and sharing their pasts—mistakes. And now that she had the hospital job locked and a clear idea of Marshall's view of her, she would spend the rest of her time here emotionally detaching herself from him.

She'd done it with her father—and it had been the hardest thing she'd ever done. The second time would be easier. But could she allow Lila, Grace, Max and Ben to be the collateral damage?

For three years she'd repeated "Let go and let God" time and again.

Maybe it was time she played out the role Belle and Marshall had put her in. She was only the paid baby nurse after all.

She had a feeling it was going to be another lousy Christmas, and she'd had twenty-three of them already.

What was one more?

Next year would be different. Next year, she'd be working at the hospital and partway through the nursing program.

And she'd forget about Marshall...next year.

Chapter Eleven

❦

"They're the sweetest things I've ever seen." Amy held Lila.

"Precious!" Lexi cradled Max.

Ainsley, holding Ben and Grace, grinned as the ladies oohed and aahed over the quadruplets. The photographer had finished packing her equipment, and Belle chatted with the redhead as she prepared to leave.

"I think my favorite was the one where they were lined up on the fluffy blanket under the Christmas tree…" Amy bit her knuckle, shaking her head. "I can't wait to see the entire set when they're developed."

"Me, too." Ainsley glanced at Belle, who'd just joined them. Belle had been gracious and pleasant to Amy and Lexi ever since they'd arrived. She'd thanked them for the casseroles they brought. She also hadn't said one word to Ainsley all day.

"Well, as much as I hate to leave these little dumplings, I have to get back." Lexi caressed Max's head. "Where should I put him?"

"Um…" Belle had a panicked air about her, but she led her to the bouncy seats. "Just put him in there. It's about time for the babies to eat."

Ainsley almost snorted. Belle said it as if she was on top of their feedings, not Ainsley. Well, tonight, the woman was in for a surprise.

Amy set Lila in a bouncy seat, and Ainsley strapped Ben and Grace into theirs, as well. Then she followed them to the front door.

"Lexi, thank you for setting this up," Ainsley said. "And, Amy, thanks for coming."

Belle was at their heels. "Yes, thank you for everything."

Lexi and Amy hugged Belle and Ainsley, then left.

As soon as the door shut, Belle started heading to her room. Ainsley glared at her retreating figure. She checked her watch. After six o'clock. Quitting time.

"I'll see you tomorrow, Belle." She put her shoes on.

Belle spun around. "What are you talking about? The babies need to be fed."

"It's fifteen minutes past quitting time."

"It won't take long to warm their bottles and—"

"Yep. It won't take long for you to feed them. Oh, and, by the way, you should really decorate the Christmas tree. Good night." With sure strides, she went through the kitchen and out the back door.

Belle opened it behind her. "Get back here!"

Ainsley lifted her hand in a backward wave and didn't stop until she reached her cabin. She frowned at the cabin next door. Marshall hadn't stopped by the main house at his regular time. And dinner with him was clearly out after their argument last night.

She went inside her cabin and changed into her favorite sweatpants and a pale pink sweatshirt. She didn't need Marshall to entertain her. She'd make a grilled cheese and come up with a list of everything she needed to do for the holidays.

After eating the sandwich, she curled up on the couch with a blanket and a notepad. She hadn't bought Tara a gift yet. Maybe on Sunday she'd pop into the mercantile Belle had mentioned that had cute gifts. And she wanted to get each of the babies a present, too. Maybe a keepsake. Did anyone in town make personalized ornaments? She'd have to check.

She couldn't think of anything else left to do.

Besides making the gingerbread ornaments, watching her favorite movies, buying a few gifts and going to church on Christmas Eve, she didn't have any other holiday traditions.

She took a candy cane down from the tree and sucked on the peppermint. Tasted like Christmas. Her thoughts drifted to her dad.

She used to buy him gifts. And he'd open them on Christmas morning and thank her, hug her and she'd feel like everything would be all right. But it never lasted. The good mood usually collapsed hours later when he cracked open his first beer.

Where was her dad now?

Did he regret not seeing her? Did he even care that she'd left?

What did he do on Christmas?

Loneliness draped over her like a lead blanket. She got up and made herself a cup of tea. A thump, thump on the door made her jump.

She opened it, and her heart beat faster.

Marshall.

"Can I come in?" Marshall stood on her doorstep, his nerves jangling worse than Raleigh's key ring to the outbuildings. The past twenty-four hours had been eating him alive. He had to apologize.

She didn't answer, just opened the door wider

and stepped back. He entered, and she returned to the couch, looking young and beautiful and miserable as she pulled the cream blanket over her legs.

"I'm sorry, Ainsley."

She didn't answer.

He forced his feet forward and stood before her. "What I said last night was unforgivable. I know how much you care about the babies. I know how hard you work. You've been generous with your time in countless ways, and I deserve a boot in the rear for my stupid words. You're a good person. One of the best I've ever met. And I hate that I hurt you."

A tiny sigh escaped her lips, and it was the saddest sound he'd heard in ages. He dropped his forehead to his hand. What was he doing? He'd messed up too badly. He couldn't expect her to forgive him.

"Thank you, Marshall. Apology accepted."

He snapped his head up. "Just like that?"

She nodded, but her eyes were still melancholy.

"I wish I could go back and shut my dumb mouth." He'd give about anything to see her smile.

"It's okay, really." She tucked her hair behind her ear.

"No, it's not. I can see you're upset." He sat

next to her on the couch. Took her hand in his. "I'm really sorry."

"I know." Her voice cracked. Was she going to cry? She looked away. "I'm just down tonight."

"Why?" He caressed her hand with his thumb.

"A couple of reasons. Nothing, really."

He turned her chin to face him. "It's something. Tell me. I don't like to see you this way."

She swallowed. "I guess it's lonely sometimes."

"What is?" He couldn't tear his gaze away from her lips.

"Being me."

He took in her silky blond hair, big shining eyes, the pastel sweatshirt she wore and pink socks peeking out below the blanket. He wanted to take her loneliness and fling it out the window. This exquisite woman with a heart bigger than the Wyoming sky meant so much to him.

He loved her.

His lungs locked up.

Love? No. Uh-uh.

She toyed with the blanket. "I try not to think of my dad, but I wonder what he's doing now. Who will he spend Christmas with? Will he be sober long enough to know it's a holiday? Is he..." Worry pinched her face.

He wanted to kiss her. Take away her pain. But he wouldn't. Couldn't.

"Do you have any way of reaching him?" he asked.

"Yes and no." She rocked back and forth slightly. "He checks in with two ranchers from time to time. They promised to call me if anything were to happen."

He hadn't considered her father still weighed on her mind. She'd made it seem like she'd cut ties and that was that.

He should have known better. Even after his mother betrayed him, he'd hoped she would come to Yearling Group Home and bring him back to live with them. He'd indulged in so many fantasies where she'd fall to her knees and apologize, beg him to forgive her. But she'd never even visited.

"I don't expect you to believe me, but I understand that kind of loneliness."

She met his eyes then, and a spark shimmered. "I know. I believe you."

He pulled her into his arms and held her tightly. Her hair tickled his cheek, and he knew he'd never forget the way she felt. Everything about her was soft, and if he had his way, he'd keep her in his arms forever.

She eased out of the hug, her face inches from his.

Slowly, he brought his lips closer, never breaking eye contact. Her pupils widened. And he pressed his lips to hers.

Peppermint. She tasted like a candy cane.

She tentatively returned his kiss, and he sensed her courage and longing. Or maybe the longing was his, because he'd never needed a woman the way he did her.

He broke away from the kiss and scrambled to his feet.

He could long for her, love her even, but he couldn't need her.

"I'm… I… I didn't mean to…" He turned his back to her. How could he have done something so stupid? It was bad enough he loved her. But to kiss her? *Dumb, dumb, dumb.*

"We can't." She'd stood, too, and she walked in jerky movements over to her Christmas tree. "I didn't mean to either."

Why wasn't relief plunging through him? Why did he feel so let down?

"Uh, I'll get out of here." He knew his face was flaming red. "Do you still want a ride Sunday? I mean, I won't…" He was losing it. He hadn't stammered this much in years.

"Yeah. Sure." She spun to face him, her eyes wide. "Oh, wait. I was going to do some Christmas shopping after. I'd better drive myself."

"Oh, okay. No problem." He hurried to the door. "I'll see you later."

He let himself out and practically ran to his cabin.

What a colossal mistake.

He'd made some big ones in his life, but this ranked right up there.

Kissing Ainsley, loving her, was out of the question.

He let the cold seep into his bones as he stared at his door. Then he slowly turned, taking in the stillness of the winter night.

It gave him no peace.

The wide-open spaces imprisoned him.

His heart did, too. How was he going to stop loving Ainsley? He had no future with her. If he was honest with himself, he didn't have much of a future at all.

What a terrible development.

Ainsley brought her fingers to her lips as soon as Marshall left. She wanted to memorize his kiss—the faint taste of mouthwash, the undemanding pressure of his lips against hers. She'd sensed something hidden inside him—the longing to be valued and understood. Everything she needed to know about Marshall Graham, she'd learned from his kiss.

Had he ever been cherished? Loved?

She didn't think so.

But whether he knew it or not, that had changed. Because she loved him. Cherished him.

But she couldn't love Marshall. She had plans. Dreams. Life goals—in Laramie. Not here.

And it didn't take a genius to understand Marshall would never love her the way she loved him. She padded back to the couch and snatched up her notepad and pen.

Her only option was to get through the next couple of weeks with her heart guarded.

She wasn't letting her dreams slip away this time.

Chapter Twelve

Seven days. That's how long she and Marshall had been tiptoeing around the fact they'd kissed. And with the holidays approaching, Ainsley's feelings for Marshall weren't her most pressing problem. Belle's erratic behavior was. Ainsley was almost out of options on how to help the woman. Her last resort seemed to be the only way forward.

It meant she'd have to talk to Raleigh. If he couldn't convince Belle to see a doctor, well, Ainsley would guide him through the baby's schedules, teach him the basics and hope he bonded with them enough to make up for Belle's emotional distance.

Ainsley took Ben's empty bottle and checked the other three. Max was almost asleep. Lila had quit after downing half her bottle, but Grace was still working on hers. Ainsley went to the kitchen and peered out the window. Marshall would be here any minute. *Good.* She had a favor to ask.

She'd kept quiet, expected nothing, since their kiss, but she'd ask him for this. She'd better get her coat and boots ready. Moments later, she checked the window again.

There he was. Relief seeped into her veins.

She met him at the back entrance, where he was stomping his boots.

"Oh." He sounded surprised. "Hi."

"Hi." How she wished he would take her into his arms again! She glanced over her shoulder, then shrugged into her coat. "Would you watch the babies for me for fifteen minutes?"

"Of course. Why?" He looked around. "Where's Belle?"

"She drove into town earlier. She's picking up gifts."

He crossed his arms over his chest. "What's going on? You're acting funny."

She didn't bother denying it. Belle worried her more and more.

"I'm going out to find Raleigh. I have to talk to him."

"About what?"

She couldn't read his face, but from his tone, he clearly didn't like her talking to the man.

"Isn't it obvious? The babies and your sister." She didn't mean to sound so exasperated, but really? "Belle's been very volatile this week. She's either staring into space, walking on the treadmill or yelling at me."

"What do you think *he's* going to do?" Marshall's brows drew together.

"I don't know, but I can tell you what I'm *not* going to do." She took a deep breath, slipping her feet into her boots. "I'm not going to assume Belle will take care of these infants when I leave. That means I need to get Raleigh up to speed on the babies' schedule. As soon as possible."

She kept her eyes steady as she met his glare.

"Do you really—" His eyes had darkened.

"What? Think it's necessary? Think Raleigh will agree? Whatever you were going to say, save it. I care about four things—and they're all bundled up in the living room. Now, will you stay with them or not? I already texted him I'd meet him at the stable."

He gave her a curt nod. "Belle won't listen to him about seeing a doctor either."

"I have to try." She fled out the door. It was a cold, blustery day, and she clasped her coat collar tightly as she fought her way through the wind to the stables.

Raleigh met her at the door and ushered her into his small office. He offered her a stool, but she declined. She stood near the doorway. Various clipboards hung in a straight line from nails in the wall. The counter was tidy, too.

"Thanks for meeting with me." She tried to calm her nerves. Over the years she'd learned to sandwich difficult topics in between positive updates. Hopefully, Raleigh wouldn't be too dismissive. Or angry.

"Sure thing. What can I do for you?" He leaned against the counter, giving her his full attention.

"Well, first of all, the babies are wonderful. They all seem to be growing fine and have taken to the schedule better than I'd hoped."

A proud smile appeared and his blue eyes crinkled. "They are cute. Gonna be good ranch helpers when they get older."

"Yes, I think they will be." Now for the more difficult part. "I'm a little concerned."

"Is it Lila? She's too small, isn't she?" He took off his work gloves and slapped them against his thigh. "I try to get her to eat at night…"

"No, nothing like that. Lila will be fine. She's just smaller and eats less. That's okay. I'm concerned about Belle."

A curtain closed across his face, and his eyes took on a glacier chill. "I don't know what to do about her. I'm new at this parenting thing, and I've never been around babies. I didn't expect her to be so…"

She waited a second. "Ambivalent?"

"Angry." He looked to the side. "I can't do anything right."

"Yeah, I can't either." She kept her chin high. "But I don't think she can help it. She's displaying multiple symptoms of postpartum depression. I've talked to her about it. She wasn't receptive to going to the doctor. I thought maybe if you mentioned it, she'd be more reasonable."

"Me?" He choked out a bitter laugh. "Why don't you ask Mr. Hero in there? She relies on Marshall for everything, anyhow."

Ouch. She hadn't realized Marshall and Raleigh's relationship had become so strained.

"I've asked him on more than one occasion."

Horses nickered nearby. Typical scents of animals and straw wafted her way. She could tell Raleigh was grappling with his thoughts, so she didn't move.

He sighed. "You think it's serious, don't you?"

"I do." She forced her gaze to stay steady as he searched her eyes. "I'm leaving soon. When I'm not here, what do you think will happen?"

"I want to believe Belle will take care of the young'uns, but I don't really believe it. I think everything will go right back to the way it was before you arrived. Marshall will ditch his duties and be taking care of the babies all day. I

didn't hire him to babysit. I hired him to ranch."
He balled his hands down by his sides.

Poor Marshall. Raleigh didn't seem to understand the only reason Marshall worked there was to help Belle. It wasn't as if Marshall had needed a job or loved ranching.

"If he didn't go over there, what do you think would happen?"

"I don't know." His posture eased, and he uncurled his fingers. "Belle will do the right thing."

"And if she doesn't?" She hated pressing, but she had to secure the babies' care, one way or another.

"I can't bear to think little Lila might not get fed." He made a choking sound and quickly covered it with a cough. It broke her heart seeing him so anguished. "Or any of them for that matter."

She wanted to reassure him Belle would step up to the task, but she couldn't.

With another heavy sigh, he shook his head. "What do you suggest?"

"I think she'd be more receptive to going to the doctor if you asked her. I've seen you with her. You have the touch, and she loves you. She wants to make you happy."

Relief softened his face.

"I also think you should try to hire someone to come in part-time to help her once I'm gone. Either mornings or afternoons, but not both. Belle needs to be hands-on with their care, at least for part of the day."

"What if I hire someone, and Belle doesn't take care of them when the babysitter isn't around?"

"Then you'll have to take care of them," she said quietly. "I'd like for you to come over for a few hours each afternoon next week. I'll show you everything you need to know—how to give them baths, getting them ready in the morning, bottle prep, how to calm them, laundry."

He gulped. "Why me?"

"Because you're their daddy, and they need you. I know how devoted you are to this ranch. You're responsible for the calves and all your cattle. And maybe you think Belle should be responsible for the quadruplets the same way. But right now, she can't. Your babies need you even more than the livestock does, Raleigh. Do you really want Marshall caring for the children instead of you?"

"I never thought of it like that." Worry lines creased his forehead, but he nodded. "How long would I have to come over?"

"Can you get away for two hours? Starting Monday?"

He bit the corner of his lip.

"The ranch will be okay for two hours." She

clasped her hands. "Having you at the house might even push Belle to get involved more... and I think it would help you to resent Marshall less."

"I don't resent him," he said too quickly.

She wrapped her coat more tightly around her body. "I've got to get back. Thanks for listening. And for caring."

"Ainsley?"

She paused.

"Thanks for taking care of my children."

"You're welcome. It's been an honor."

A blast of wind hit her as she left the stables, but she barely felt it. She'd accomplished what she'd set out to do. She just hoped it worked. It would be hard enough leaving soon. She couldn't bear to go without feeling assured the babies were being taken care of by at least one of their parents.

"Why is she taking so long?" Marshall held both twin boys on his lap. "Not that I don't love you two. I do. You know it."

Ben smiled at him. Marshall's mouth dropped open. He'd smiled!

He couldn't wait to tell Ainsley.

"You guys like me, don't you?" He kissed their foreheads. "I expect to see more smiles, Ben, and, you, Max, need to get on board, too."

He craned his neck to address the girls on their activity mats on the floor. "Same for you, little ladies. I want everyone to smile for Uncle Marshall."

They gurgled and stared at the toys dangling above them. Max rolled his lips, his tongue darting out.

"Your mama is going to be so…" He frowned. *So…what?* Belle showed no interest in these kids. Would she care Ben had smiled? Would she watch the other babies in breathless anticipation of catching their first smiles? He didn't think she would. Maybe he was wrong.

As if on cue, Belle breezed through the front door, her arms loaded with packages. She kicked the door closed. "Oh, hey, Marsh, would you give me a hand?"

He looked at the babies he held, then back at her. "My hands are kind of full at the moment."

She set the bags in the hallway and took off her coat. "Where's Ainsley?"

He almost blurted out that she was talking to Raleigh, but he doubted that would go over well. "She'll be right back."

"You mean she just left you with the children?"

The statement struck him as odd. Belle left Ainsley with them all the time. She left *him* with them, too.

"Hey, Ben smiled at me." He hitched his head for her to come over.

"Oh. Good." Her eyelashes fluttered. "I'd better put this stuff away."

"Don't you want to come over and see if he does it again?"

She picked up the bags and made her way through the living room. "I'll see it later."

"Belle…"

"Not now, Marshall!" She slammed her door.

He took in the living room, the happy babies, the undecorated tree, and a wave of sadness crushed him.

She was missing it. All of it. His sister was missing this once-in-a-lifetime experience. And she didn't know it. Didn't care.

The back door opened. A few minutes later Ainsley appeared, her cheeks bright pink from the cold.

"Thanks," she said. "I can take it from here."

He rose, hoisting the babies with him, then setting them on their activity mats next to the girls.

"What did he say?" He wanted to get closer to her, to take her by the hand and press his lips to the back of it. He wanted to ask her to forgive him.

He wanted her to stay.

"He agreed. He'll be coming up to the house for a few hours each afternoon next week."

Marshall was taken aback. Raleigh—the tough rancher—was coming over to help with the babies?

"What about…?" He shifted his eyes to the hall where Belle's room was.

She shrugged. "I don't know. He seemed open to talking to her. It's a start."

He didn't know what to say. So many thoughts ran through his head. He wanted to relieve the pressure on his heart and tell her the truth. That he thought about her day and night and couldn't seem to stop. That he'd fallen for her. And life on Dushane Ranch was going to be lonely and unbearable after she left.

But he just stood there, his thumbs hooked in his belt loops.

"Like I said, you can take off." She pushed past him to get to the babies, but he caught her by the arm and lightly caressed her sweater with his thumb.

"Why don't you come over tonight for dinner?"

She hesitated. "I don't know if that's a good idea."

"Look, I'm not going to attack you or anything." He tried to laugh, but it fell flat. "I miss our time together. I know you have to leave, but in the meantime, can we go back to the way it was?"

She licked her lips, dropping her gaze. Then she met his eyes. "Sure. Why not?"

He should be glad, but she seemed less than thrilled at the prospect.

She got on her knees to engage with the infants, and he couldn't help but watch her for a few moments. She'd been so good to the children, to him, to his sister and even to Raleigh. She was the most giving, brave woman he knew.

And he could feel her emotionally distancing herself from him more and more with each passing day.

"I'll see you tonight." He waited, hoping she'd give him that big smile he'd grown to love, but she merely glanced up and nodded.

As he powered through the wind, he tried to ignore the emptiness in his heart. It wasn't as if he'd expected Ainsley to share his feelings. And it was better she didn't. They didn't have a future.

Several cows lowed from the nearby pasture. *I feel the same way, fellas.* It wasn't just Ainsley getting him down. He missed his sister—the sassy, fun, sweet woman who'd gone missing ever since the babies arrived. He didn't know how to get her back.

Was he even trying? Ainsley was the one

bending over backward to help Belle. And Belle didn't appreciate it at all. Did he for that matter?

He moved faster and almost bumped into Raleigh in the barn.

"Sorry, man, didn't see you there." Marshall stepped out of the way.

"Not a problem." Raleigh didn't make eye contact.

Marshall took a deep breath. He wanted to help, too. And not by sticking a bandage over the problem.

"Raleigh?"

"Yeah?" He looked vulnerable. Marshall had never seen this side of his brother-in-law.

"Ainsley said you'll be helping with the babies next week."

He flushed. "That's right."

"Leave me a list each day before you go, and I'll make sure your work out here gets done."

His jaw dropped. "That would be a big load off my mind."

"I know it would." Marshall shifted from one foot to the other. "Can I ask you a favor?"

"Shoot."

"I don't know how much Belle has told you about our childhood."

"She's told me enough." His tone hardened.

"Just be gentle with her, okay? We both got knocked around as kids, and I can't speak for her, but I know arguments bring out parts of me I wish they wouldn't."

"I'll take that into consideration." Raleigh strode away.

Marshall watched him, not knowing if he'd said the right thing or the wrong one. It was a sad day when he couldn't trust his own mind anymore.

He didn't know who he was. Belle's brother. The quadruplets' uncle. Raleigh's ranch hand.

None of them seemed to add up.

His cell phone rang, and he answered it. "Marshall Graham."

"Marshall, good to hear your voice again."

"Mr. Beatty, what a nice surprise." His mood lifted as he thought of all he'd learned from his old boss. "What can I do for you?"

"You know I don't go for formal stuff. Call me Bill. And it's funny you should ask, but Peter and I are branching out. We're opening a repair shop in Laramie, and we think you're the guy to run it for us. Of course, you'd be the head repairman, too, so it would be an increase in pay from when you last worked for us."

He almost dropped the phone. Working for the Beatty brothers again? In Laramie?

Visions of complicated machinery filled his mind. He missed the challenge. Missed the work.

Oh, man, he missed it. And to run their shop? What a privilege.

It didn't escape his attention that Laramie was where Ainsley was headed. He could picture himself getting off work and picking her up from the hospital to grab a bite to eat. Her big smile would be an everyday event for him.

A moo brought him back to reality.

"Wow, I'm honored." He tried to find a polite way to turn him down.

"You were the best we ever had, Marshall."

The words filled him with pride—not in himself—but that Mr. Beatty would think so highly of him.

"I can't tell you how much that means to me." Marshall wasn't going to beat around the bush. "I would like to say yes, but I can't. I'm not available."

"I was afraid you'd say that. Your sister is mighty blessed to have you around."

"I'm blessed to be here."

"Listen, Marshall, why don't you take the holidays to think about it? No rush."

He'd be thinking about it, all right, but only as a fantasy.

"Oh, Marge is calling. I'll be in touch." Mr. Beatty hung up before Marshall could reply.

He pocketed his phone and stared ahead at the pregnant cow confined in the barn. An endless string of days paraded before him—all the same. Chasing down sick calves. Feeding healthy cows. Tagging during calving.

What was the alternative? Sure, he could enjoy pretending life would be sugary sweet in Laramie with him fixing farm equipment and seeing Ainsley, but that's not how it would go. It would be a frantic call in the night from Belle saying one of the babies was sick and she didn't know what to do. Or if she didn't call, he'd worry something else was wrong. There would be no winning.

Where did he belong?

Here?

In Laramie?

At least here he could live with a clear conscience. He'd be available at a moment's notice if anything were to go wrong.

Living on Dushane Ranch was the right choice.

Ainsley had been counting down the hours until she could eat dinner with Marshall, and the time had finally arrived. Ever since talking to Raleigh earlier, she'd felt more peaceful about leaving the babies after the holidays. But leaving Marshall? She didn't feel peace about it at all.

She took a minute to get her bearings before knocking on Marshall's door. She'd done so well pushing away her feelings for him. Since she'd barely seen him this week, she'd done her best to pretend she didn't love him. She'd failed.

But she'd keep trying…after tonight.

Marshall opened the door, and she just stood there staring at him. His stubble was trimmed, his brown eyes gleaming, and his flannel shirt and jeans beckoned her to come in. She did.

An awkward silence fell.

"Should I—"

"Why don't you—"

They laughed. He looked flushed. Excited.

"Everything okay?" she asked.

"Yes. Let me get the food." He pulled chicken breasts out of the oven and placed them on a platter. Then he tossed a hot pad on the table and brought a pot of pasta over.

She resumed their previous routine and took the silverware and napkins out of the drawer. Then she set two plates at the table, took a seat and watched him serve the meal.

"Something good happened to you today," she teased, waving her finger. "I can tell."

He raised his eyebrows, grinning. "My old boss called. Wants me to come work for him."

"Marshall, that's terrific! Would you move back to Cheyenne?"

"Not exactly. They're opening a new shop in Laramie and want me to run it, but I said no."

No? Her joy for him popped. "Why? I know how much you loved your job."

"Doesn't matter. It was nice to be asked, though." He gestured to their plates. "Why don't you pray before everything gets cold?"

Frowning, she bowed her head and said the prayer. When she finished, she watched Marshall cut his food into precise bites. Was he declining the job because it was in Laramie, near her? Or was it something else?

Of course it was something else—it was Belle. Always Belle.

"You can have your own life, you know." She used her least threatening voice. The one she wished someone would have used on her when she was convinced she had to keep her dad's life together. "It doesn't have to be either-or."

"I'm not following you." He briefly met her eyes but quickly refocused on his food.

"I attended Al-Anon meetings for over two years. It helped me understand myself. I believed I was responsible for my father. I wanted to save him. I thought if I could control everything, he'd finally quit drinking. But I wasn't responsible for him, I couldn't save him, and the more I tried to control everything, the worse he drank."

"Okay." He sniffed, fork in hand. "I don't see what this has to do with me."

How could she get through to him? In a way he'd actually accept?

"Whether you're working on Dushane Ranch or living in Laramie, Belle is going to go through whatever she's going to go through."

"You lost me."

"I guess I'm saying you can support and love Belle from Cheyenne or Laramie as good as you can here."

"Let's drop it." He pushed away from the table slightly.

Frustrated, she sighed. Why did she always jump into situations where her help wasn't wanted?

Was she still in saving mode? Saving Belle. Saving the quads. Saving Marshall.

Hadn't she learned the hard way the only person she was responsible for was herself? She took a bite of the pasta, barely tasting it, but trying to reclaim the good mood. "Mmm. This is delicious."

"Look, Ainsley, I don't mean to sound like a grizzly. It's been an odd day. I appreciate all you're doing with Raleigh and Belle. I offered to do Raleigh's afternoon chores next week while you show him the baby ropes."

"You did?" Her spirits brightened.

"Yeah. It's the least I can do. You might not

believe me, but I really do want Belle to get better. Did I tell you Ben smiled at me earlier?"

"And I missed it? Aw! Tell me everything. What were you doing? Did the others smile, too?"

"Just him, and it tickled me. Cutest thing I'd ever seen…"

Ainsley kept her spirits up with Marshall throughout the rest of the meal. Her heart kept hitching, wishing he would change his mind about taking the job. Wishing he would put himself first and get off the ranch. But she knew he wasn't going to.

She'd enjoy him as much as she could before driving back to Laramie. The memories of these nights would keep her warm whenever life was cold. She just hoped she'd be able to keep a level head when it came time to leave. Giving up her dreams for a man overly devoted to his sister would never make her happy.

Chapter Thirteen

"This baby is slipperier than a wet calf. How am I supposed to keep her from drowning?" Raleigh's scared, screwed-up face was priceless. Ainsley couldn't help it—she laughed.

She pointed to the washcloth near his right hand. "Just keep a firm grasp under her shoulders and use your other hand to clean her. Gently."

This was their fourth day of baby training, and he was getting the hang of it. She'd been trying to get him to bathe the dears all week, and today he'd finally agreed. They stood in the dining room, where she'd placed towels on the table, then the baby bathtub on top of the towels. At this rate, Raleigh would be more than comfortable taking on any baby task after Ainsley left. With less than two weeks before the end of the year, it left enough time for him to gain confidence in his growing baby skills.

"Go ahead and talk to her." Ainsley stood to the left. "She wants to hear her daddy's voice."

"Ah, okay…you're getting clean, Grace." He sounded like he was giving orders to one of the cowboys.

"Um, I was thinking maybe a little more, you know, cutesy? Baby talk."

His neck grew red and he flashed her a glare, but he bravely returned to Grace. "How do you like your bath, sweetheart?"

"Much better." She pretended to clap. He gave her a resigned look.

Grace splashed her legs and blew a raspberry.

"See? She loves it. Keep talking to her."

"Who's the little cutie?" Raleigh cooed. He quickly washed her body. Then he turned to Ainsley. "Now what?"

"You're going to lift her out of the tub and set her on the towel I laid out. Then wrap her up, take her to the changing table and put a new outfit on her. I'll get Lily ready for her bath."

"Thank you." He nodded, his throat working. "I don't suppose there's any way we could convince you to stay, is there?"

Why his words touched her, she couldn't say. But the tears pressing against the backs of her eyes couldn't be denied. She was really going to miss this family.

"I can't stay, Raleigh, but it means a lot to me that you asked."

A door slamming made them both jump. Grace's startled face quivered and she began to cry.

Belle stormed into the dining room, popped her hands on her hips and glared at Ainsley.

"How dare you!" The words were low, venomous.

Ainsley tried to figure out what Belle was upset about. She'd been hot and cold all week. One minute yelling at Ainsley for no reason, the next sidling up to Raleigh. It had been extremely strange.

"You came in here and acted all innocent." Belle advanced on her, finger pointing. "But I'm on to you."

"What are you talking about?" Ainsley handed Raleigh a pacifier. He held Grace wrapped in a towel to his chest and gave her the binkie to quiet her.

"It's bad enough you're turning my babies against me—"

"Stop it, Belle." Raleigh gave his wife a warning look.

"Don't tell me to stop." She pointed her finger at him. "You're as bad as she is."

"I've never tried to turn your children against you." Ainsley stayed calm. Was it even possible for someone to turn tiny infants against someone? She doubted it, but Belle was clearly in a bizarre state of mind.

Belle flicked her hair behind her shoulder. "And now you're trying to steal my husband from me, too."

"What?" Ainsley and Raleigh said simultaneously.

"Don't act like you don't know what I'm talking about. I know you met him at the stables. I found the texts. And all week he's been here *helping*—" she jerked her fingers into air quotes "—with the babies. You both disgust me."

"Those are ugly accusations, Belle." Raleigh shifted Grace to his other arm. His cheekbones jutted against tight skin.

"Yeah, the truth hurts, doesn't it?" She glowered at him like a bomb about to explode.

Ainsley stood as tall as she could muster. This was her thanks for nonstop infant care? Being accused of trying to steal Belle's husband? Hurt and anger pooled in her gut.

"I texted Raleigh because I'm leaving soon, and someone will have to take care of these children." Ainsley leveled her with a stare. "These babies deserve to have loving, hands-on parents."

"Liar!" Belle shouted. "You wanted him here

for yourself. You're a terrible person. I can't believe I trusted you with my children. You hate them. And you hate me!"

Ainsley debated her next move. She would not engage with this woman any longer. And this environment had grown too toxic for her to stay.

"I don't want you near my babies or my husband!" Belle yelled. "You're fired. Get out!"

Ainsley blinked her eyes wide as her mouth dropped open. All she could do was shake her head back and forth. Was this really happening?

"That's enough, Belle!"

All three of them turned to look at the kitchen. Marshall stood at the edge of the dining room. His legs were wide and his arms locked down by his sides, his hands balled into fists. His entire body seemed to throb with energy.

"Apologize to Ainsley. Right now."

"If you think I'm ever apologizing to that home wrecker, you're out of your mind!"

Marshall could hardly control his temper as anger pumped adrenaline through his veins. He'd walked in as Belle accused Ainsley of trying to steal Raleigh from her. What a joke. And then to accuse Ainsley of hating the babies...

"If it wasn't for Ainsley, these children you wanted so desperately wouldn't be as healthy and happy as they are today."

"I should have known you'd take *her* side." Belle spun on her heel to flee to her room, but Marshall ran over and blocked the hallway.

"She has done nothing but sacrifice for you and your children, and you are really going to stand here and say such nasty things?"

Belle tried to push him out of the way. He didn't budge. Tears began to stream down her face.

"Aw, Belle—" he took her by the biceps "—I hate seeing you like this. Something's not right. You've got to see a doctor. You need help."

"Get out," she whispered, as a sob erupted. "Get out! You aren't welcome here anymore!"

He let her go and stepped back. A lifetime of empathy for her filled him, but he couldn't make this better for her. Not this time.

"I said to get out! Both of you." She pointed to him and then to Ainsley.

Ainsley's face was pale and pinched. Marshall would do about anything to take away the pain his sister had caused her. She met his eyes briefly and gave her head a slight shake.

"Now!" Belle shook with fury, then ran to her room.

Ainsley approached Raleigh. She looked shattered as she put her hand on Grace's head. "Take care, little Gracie," she whispered. "You'll always be the one your siblings go to when they have a problem."

A lump grew in Marshall's throat. He didn't know what to do. What to say. This couldn't be happening.

"Ainsley, wait," Raleigh said. "Let me talk to her. I know she didn't mean it."

"I can't." Her voice cracked.

"Yes, you can," Marshall said. A frantic energy built inside him, like a storm gathering power. He couldn't let her go. "She'll calm down. She'll apologize."

"I'm done, Marshall." Her eyes pleaded with him to understand.

Marshall shadowed Ainsley as she padded over to the other three babies in their bouncy seats. She kissed her finger and touched Ben's cheek.

"Stay fierce, Ben. And, Max, always have his back, but don't let him get into too much trouble, okay?" She hiccuped, a trail of tears running down her cheeks. She kissed Lila's forehead. "And you, sweet sunshine, be the light."

"Ainsley…" Marshall couldn't find the words. He tried to swallow the lump in his throat. Watching her say goodbye was killing him.

She rose, wiping under her eyes with the backs of her hands. She collected her coat and hitched her chin to Raleigh, whose face was ashen. "It was good to know you. Take care of them. Please, just love them and take care of them." Her voice broke, and she ran outside.

"Wait—" Raleigh called.

But Marshall was already chasing Ainsley. He had to apologize. Had to fix this.

"Ainsley!" He caught up to her as she reached her cabin. "What happened back there—"

"It's okay. I'll be fine. And the babies will, too. Raleigh knows their schedule, and he can handle it."

"That's not what I meant."

"I don't know what you want me to say." Her eyes were filled with anguish. "I have to go."

"You can't leave." He opened his hands, wanting to pull her to him, stroke her hair and promise her he'd make it all better. "Can we go inside and talk about it?"

Her shoulders drooped as she sighed. She opened the door and let him in. They took off their coats. She took a seat on the couch, and he sat on the chair. The ticking of the clock on the wall echoed.

"I'm sorry." He leaned forward, knees spread, hands clasped between them. "I don't know why Belle said all those things."

"It's not your place to apologize for her." She had a fragile air, like a porcelain doll.

"Maybe not, but after all you've done for us—"

"Us?" A frown formed. "I was doing it for her. And the babies. I wanted them to have a better life than I did. Parents who cared. And after the way she just yelled at you, I can't believe you're still putting her in the category of *us*. You need to get away from here, Marshall."

He bristled. Maybe he deserved that, but he had to believe it was the aftereffects of her anger. "My sister will always be on my team. I'm not cutting her out of my life."

She looked like she'd been slapped. "You mean the way I cut my father out of mine?"

"No, of course not." He leaned back, not knowing how to talk to her. "It's just…different."

The gleam in her eyes sent warning signals to his brain.

"Take the job in Laramie, Marshall. Do what you love. Leave this ranch. Your sister doesn't want you here, anyhow."

He was having a hard time getting air to his lungs. *Leave the ranch?* "You know I can't do that. Not now."

"Especially now." She stood. "Take a chance."

He gaped at her. She walked over and held her hands out, drawing him out of the chair. He wanted to sink his hands into her silky hair, but he stood like a statue.

"I love you, Marshall. I took one look at you

holding the twins the day I arrived, and I've been fighting a losing battle ever since. I love you, and I want you to have a good life. A full life. Your *own* life. Come to Laramie. Call your old boss and take the job."

His mind raced. She loved him? And wanted him to move? The thought was sweeter than he cared to admit.

But it was unthinkable.

"I left my sister at the most vulnerable time of her life, and I barely had a relationship with her for five years. Things went bad for her. And I wasn't around." His throat grew tighter and tighter.

"I know. I get it. I do." She squeezed his hands, staring up at him with so much love it took his breath away. "But she's got Raleigh now. And the babies. And she's grown up. This isn't the same."

He pulled out of her grasp. He couldn't make her understand. "I can't leave her. Not now. Not until she's better."

"Not until she's better," Ainsley said softly. "I used to tell myself I'd go to college when my dad was better. I'd find a boyfriend when he was better. My life would start when he was better. But he never did get better."

"It's not the same."

"Your sister and my dad aren't the same. You're right about that. But you and me—the way I was—that's the same. I put my life on hold to fix my dad. And you're putting yours on hold to fix your sister. It's called codependency, Marshall, and I don't play that game anymore."

He massaged the back of his neck. "I disagree. I don't see what's wrong with being there for her."

She stepped closer to him and placed her hand on his cheek. "I know you don't."

He covered her hand with his, leaning his cheek into it. "Stay. Through the holidays. She'll get over it. She'll calm down…"

She slipped her hand from under his and took two steps back, shaking her head.

"You can't leave, and I can't stay." She stood tall. "Do you know how much I wanted to be number one in my father's life? More than anything. But alcohol always held the top spot. And here I am in love with a man who will always put his sister first. I've been a distant second my entire life. I'm worth more than that. I'm not staying here."

"It wouldn't be like that."

"It already is. You know your way out." She crossed her arms over her chest and stared at him through those green-gold eyes. They were strong, determined, beautiful.

He opened his mouth to say something, but she walked to the door. With each step a piece of his heart broke off.

"Take care of yourself, Marshall." She held the door open, and he had no choice but to grab his coat and leave. The door shut behind him as soon as he crossed the threshold.

The events of the past hour swirled. He had to do something. If he made Belle apologize...

Nothing would change.

If he went back in there and told Ainsley he loved her...

Nothing would change.

If he waited an hour, would things cool down? Could he reason with her?

He stood on her porch, the cold seeping into his bones.

He needed to tell her he loved her. He couldn't let her walk out of his life.

What if he took the job and left Belle to—

No, I can't. I can't live with myself if Belle's life falls apart again. This wasn't supposed to happen!

He faced the door and closed his eyes, whispering, "I love you. Don't make me choose. Don't leave."

Then he bowed his head and plodded next door.

Telling her he loved her wouldn't change anything.

She was right. She deserved to be number one, and he'd filled that spot long ago.

Chapter Fourteen

Ainsley shoved the last of her sweaters into the suitcase, then looked around. The bed was made. Closet empty. Bathroom cleared. Sink wiped out. She zipped the suitcase and brought it into the living room to stand next to the others. Her laptop, tote bag and chargers were packed away. The only things remaining were the contents of the fridge, which she was leaving, and the Christmas decorations. She contemplated leaving the decorations the way they were. Let Marshall or Belle or Raleigh clean them up behind her. But that's not how Ainsley Draper did things. No, she finished what she started.

She found a large bowl in the kitchen and took all of the gingerbread ornaments from the tree. She refused to think about how she'd baked them with Marshall and then hung them with so much joy. Instead, she chucked them into the bowl.

She didn't bother unstringing the lights from the tree, just unplugged it, picked the entire thing up and took it straight out to her car, shoving it into the back seat.

On a surge of adrenaline, she dragged the suitcases out one by one and hauled them into the trunk. Ran a dust mop across the floor, turned off the lights and glared at the bowl of gingerbread. The birds could have them. She swiped up the bowl, ran out to the back of her cabin and flung the contents into the air. They flew, some cracking, others breaking as they landed in the snow.

The sight broke her heart even more, but she forced herself to look away and marched back into the cabin. After putting the bowl in the sink, she slipped her arms into her coat, grabbed her purse and did one more walk-through. On her way out, she paused and exhaled.

Goodbye, pretty cabin.

She blinked away tears and left. Her car started right up, and she wasted no time leaving. She tried not to look at the main house. The thought of never seeing the babies again was killing her. She'd never hold them or kiss them or change their tiny diapers.

She wouldn't see their smiles. Wouldn't be able to give them the ornaments she'd bought them.

Their sweet baby smell was gone…forever.

The car bumped and jolted as she pressed the gas, and finally, she turned onto the main road. Instead of seeing miles of pasture and distant mountains, she could see only Marshall's face.

She'd told him she loved him. And he didn't love her back.

Don't cry. Don't you dare cry, Ainsley!

All the awful things of the day flitted through her head. Belle's terrible accusations. Grace's cry when Belle stormed in. Raleigh's stricken, angry face. Marshall confronting Belle... Hearing, "You're fired." Having to say goodbye to the quadruplets.

You're stronger than the tears. You did the right thing.

Had she done the right thing, though?

Maybe Marshall had been correct to stay. To help Raleigh and Belle until she—until she what?

The woman needed professional help, not the two men in her life to tiptoe around her and pretend everything was fine.

Ainsley gripped the steering wheel and pressed the accelerator. The sooner she returned to Laramie, the sooner she could immerse herself in reality. Not the isolated atmosphere she'd been in—the one that made her doubt herself. She'd meant it when she'd told Marshall she wasn't sticking around to be number two.

Unfortunately, the only person who considered her number one was herself.

Well, that wasn't true. She was always number one in God's eyes. She sniffed.

The road to Sweet Dreams came into view. She shouldn't detour. She should stay straight and take the shortest route back to Laramie. But the tug of the town pulled her, and she made a right.

The houses on the outskirts stood close together, and soon she was rolling slowly past the cute shops and Dottie's Diner.

No more breakfasts with Amy and Lexi. No more coloring with Ruby.

No more cozy dinners and laughter and movies and happiness with Marshall.

The town faded away, and it felt as if she was saying goodbye to her entire life.

It was going to be another lonely Christmas.

Marshall heard Ainsley's car drive away, and as the crunching of her tires faded, he felt sick to his stomach. Letting her leave felt…wrong. Worse than wrong. Terrifying.

A memory latched to him, and he tried to shake it off, but it clung. It was his mother's face the night he'd tried to convince her to leave Ed. Marshall had just showed her the welts on his back and begged her to open her eyes, to see what was happening.

Horror had flashed across her face. And she'd seemed like she believed him. But then he'd blown it. He should have stopped while he'd been ahead. He'd thought telling her about Ed's inappropriate feelings for Belle would clinch it.

But something in her eyes had shut down. She'd brushed his words aside, reverted to her oblivious self, the one who refused to acknowledge what was happening in front of her. She'd turned away to keep making dinner. So he'd pressed harder. Told her he'd seen Ed standing too close to Belle, leering at her. And she'd waved him off, told him he'd misunderstood.

He'd known he was losing the battle, but had he backed off? No, he'd grabbed the knife and held it in front of her. And he'd uttered the words that had sealed his fate. "So help me, if you move us into his house, I'll kill him."

She hadn't said a word.

A pounding sound came from his cabin door, and he shook the memory away.

"Marshall? You in there?"

He swayed as he stood, the blood rushing to his head.

"Just a minute."

Something important teetered at the edge of the memory. Something having to do with Ainsley. He balled his hands into fists and pressed them to his eyes. *Forget it. Forget your mother. Forget Ainsley. Forget everything.*

"Marshall?"

He crossed the room and opened the door. Raleigh stood there. "Can I come in?"

"Yeah." He should ask how Belle was. He should be worried about the babies. But he felt empty. Done.

Raleigh headed straight to the kitchen table and took a seat. "I saw Ainsley's car drive away."

He tried to reply, but nothing came out. Thinking of her leaving choked him up too much to say a word.

"What Belle said back there..." Raleigh concentrated on the cowboy hat he crushed in his hands. "I never thought of Ainsley that way, and I know she didn't with me either."

"I know." Out of everything the man could have said, he was worried Marshall thought he'd been hitting on Ainsley? The idea was laughable. "You're not like that. You're honorable."

"I'm surprised you'd say that." Raleigh flushed and gave him a sheepish look.

"Why?" Marshall started to feel normal. And whatever had happened earlier had shifted his view of a few things, including his opinion of Raleigh. "I see how hard you work on the ranch. The way you look at Belle. You're building something here. A family. A legacy."

"Man, you're making me feel even worse." He slapped the hat against his thigh. "I owe you an apology."

He was taken aback. Raleigh apologizing?

"I've given you a hard time for months. And I haven't thanked you for stepping in with the little ones the way you did. I... I'm embarrassed to admit this, but I think I was jealous."

"Jealous?" Marshall stood behind the other chair. "Of what?"

"Your relationship with Belle."

He met his brother-in-law's blue eyes, sincere and penitent, and he understood.

"Oh."

"She relies on you. Depends on you. She knew you'd be great with the babies, and you were."

Marshall swung the chair to the side and sat. "I wasn't great with the babies, Raleigh. I was terrible."

"Pshaw," he scoffed. "You were something, Marshall. I was scared to even pick one up. Thought I'd break it. But you swung in there and held two at a time."

"Well, until Ainsley arrived, I was a mess. She was the one who got them on the schedule and made order out of the chaos."

That's what Ainsley did—made order out of

chaos—and he'd let her drive away. The beautiful woman with a heart as golden as her hair—she'd told him she loved him, and he hadn't even told her he loved her back. What did that say about him?

Maybe she was right. Was he like his mother, ignoring reality because it was convenient?

"Belle's not doing so good." Raleigh bowed his head. "I know this is a lot to ask considering all the rotten things she said, but I was hoping you would talk to her. Ainsley's right. If she doesn't get professional help, I don't know what will happen."

Marshall sprang to his feet. Belle needed him. Even Raleigh admitted it now. Marshall looked at his brother-in-law, saw the anxiety eating him alive, and he sat back down.

Oh, God, tell me Ainsley wasn't right. Am I like my mother? Looking the other way instead of doing what I should?

Shame spiraled through his core.

Dottie's smiling face crowded out his thoughts. He'd been at Yearling for a few weeks before he'd tried to run away to rescue Belle. But Big Bob had caught him. And Dottie had nudged a plate of oatmeal cookies his way and patted his shoulder. "Listen, slick," she'd said, "the good Lord sent you here for a reason."

He'd ignored her, guilt gnawing him to death

at the danger his sister was in. Then Dottie had said something she'd repeated many times over the years: "Honey, God's got this."

Raleigh thumped his knuckles on the table. "I'm sorry. I shouldn't have asked."

Marshall studied him. Really studied him. And he knew the right thing to do.

"Raleigh, she loves you. She married you. She looks at you like you're chocolate frosting on a three-layer cake. You go talk to her. She'll listen."

"I don't know, Marsh. I've never seen her like this."

"I have." Like shingles blowing off a roof, the beliefs he'd been clinging to flew away. "I'm sorry, Raleigh. I overstepped my bounds by moving here. It's your place to be Belle's rock, not mine. I hope you don't think I undermined you on purpose. I didn't."

"What are you saying?" Raleigh's face paled.

"I'm saying you're her husband. Those are your babies. And you two will work it out."

"Are you leaving?" He sounded panicked.

"I think I am." Marshall nodded absentmindedly. "I'm not meant to be a cowboy. I'm going to pack a bag and stay with my friend Wade for a while."

"But Belle will think she drove you away."

He shrugged. "Maybe she needs to deal with

the consequences this time. I love her. I'll always be here for both of you and the children, but this pickle you two are in? I don't belong in it."

Raleigh nodded, his expression growing resolved. "You're right. And Ainsley told me what I need to do. I'm getting Belle to the doctor. I'm hiring someone to help with the babies in the afternoons. And I'll do my best to take care of them in the meantime."

He stood and held out his hand.

Marshall shook it. "Call Clint or Nash if you're struggling with the quads. Lexi and Amy would be more than happy to swing by for an hour or two."

"I'll do that." Raleigh hesitated, then put his arms around him and gave him a big hug. "Thank you. For everything."

"Anytime."

Chapter Fifteen

"I miss smelling the gingerbread ornaments this year. I wish you would have brought them with you. It's not the same." Tara plugged in the Christmas tree lights in their apartment Saturday night. "Are you sure you won't come with us?"

"No thanks. You guys have fun." Ainsley didn't glance up as she scrolled through Facebook. Nothing was the same. Just thinking about the gingerbread cookies abandoned in the backyard of her little cabin on Dushane Ranch made her want to cry.

But she wouldn't.

Since arriving in Laramie a few days ago, she'd suppressed every tear. When Marshall came to mind, she blocked all thoughts of him. Busied herself by making lists and organizing her bedroom. But her room was as organized as it would ever be, and there were no lists left to make. Which left time—a yawning, endless chasm of time—on her hands.

"If you change your mind, we'll be at Tony's." Tara waved and left.

Ainsley sighed, drawing the fluffy pink throw closer to her chin. She wished her new job had started. Then she'd have something to do with herself. And she wouldn't keep thinking of the babies and wondering if Marshall was doing everything for them again. Had Belle apologized to him? And was Raleigh staying around to help, or had he escaped indefinitely to the stables?

You can't keep doing this.

She forced herself off the couch and rummaged through the cupboards. Hot chocolate—the cure for too many thoughts. As she heated the water, she couldn't help wondering what her dad was doing.

Was he in Wyoming still? Or had he headed up to Montana?

Was he okay?

The urge to check on him hit her hard. She braced her hands against the counter. *Don't get sucked into his drama again.*

Her life was better now. Being away from his addiction had allowed her to grow strong. And it wasn't as if she'd told him she never wanted to see him again. She'd simply left. She'd given him her information. He could have contacted her at any time. He'd chosen not to.

Because she'd ditched him.

Nice job, Ainsley. Way to cheer yourself up.

The microwave dinged, and she poured a cocoa packet into the mug of hot water. Returning to the living room, she stared blankly at the Christmas lights strung over the window and on the tree. She had no Christmas spirit. None. Zip.

Spotting her Bible on the end table, she reached for it. Flipped through. Leviticus? She grimaced. Not what she needed right now.

Lord, please lead me to the right verses. Show me Your comfort.

She turned to Zephaniah. Had she ever read Zephaniah? Did she want to?

Sighing, she started to close the Bible, but a word jumped out at her, and she opened it again, peering at the seventeenth verse of chapter three. "The Lord thy God in the midst of thee is mighty; he will save, he will rejoice over thee with joy; he will rest in his love, he will joy over thee with singing."

She looked around. The Lord was with her. She was snug in her warm apartment. She had a job lined up for after the holidays. She was safe and had a really good friend in Tara.

What did she have to complain about? Not much.

She'd get over Marshall.

Someday.

God, I know I did the right thing. If I would have stayed, I would have been enabling Marshall, the way I did my dad. And I would have lost respect for him. I couldn't take being treated like dirt by Belle anymore either. It's better this way. Isn't it?

She thought of all the meals Marshall had cooked for her. The way he loved the babies and dived in to help her with them whenever possible. The things he'd told her about his childhood. She understood why he was so blind about Belle. She'd been the same way about her father for most of her life.

But Marshall deserved better. He should be working at a job he loved. And if he wanted to help his sister, it should be appreciated by her, not expected.

Oh, God, please get through to him. Make him see he needs his own life. Please, help him break free from the chains of guilt tying him down.

Emotions clogged her throat. She tried to sip her hot chocolate, but couldn't.

And, God, while I'm praying, please open

Belle's heart to admit she needs help. Guide her to be a wonderful mommy to the quadruplets. And kiss each one of them for me. Keep them strong and healthy.

There was another name calling out for her to pray over, but the thought of it was frightening. Her dad was so heavy on her heart. What if she prayed and God asked her to do something dangerous? If she prayed for her father, if she reached out to him, would she get drawn back into being his keeper?

Lord, it's been so long. So terribly long since I've seen him. I don't know what to do. Hug him for me and keep him safe.

Thinking of her father's hugs ripped a tear from her eyes. When he was sober, he was so easy to love. But when he wasn't? He was impossible.

There was no fighting the tears. They leaked out one by one.

I miss you, Dad.

She tried to think of all the Al-Anon sayings she'd memorized, but none of them made sense right now. She thought of Marshall, who couldn't seem to move past the horror of the years he'd missed out on being with Belle and worrying about her. It made sense he was terrified of missing out on more.

Would she spend the rest of her life estranged from her father?

She didn't want that. She wanted a happy medium—to communicate with her father without being responsible for him.

Jesus, if You could come down as a helpless baby and live a perfect life all the while knowing You would be crucified before rising from the dead for me, then I can forgive my father. Lord, I forgive him, and I'm asking You to forgive him, too. Forgive him for all the times he neglected me, yelled at me, let me down and stole from me. Forgive him for all of it.

Her heart squeezed and emotions burned. And something shifted inside her soul. Forgiving her father wasn't the same as reverting back to their previous relationship. It was…freedom. If she never saw her father again, she'd be okay.

But…she wanted to see him.

Okay, Lord, I'll try to find him tomorrow, but I'm trusting You to keep me safe. Don't let me throw away my goals because I feel bad for Dad.

And what about Marshall? What was she supposed to do about him?

I know I'm asking for a lot, Lord, but I want so much for Marshall. I want him to be happy. And if he ever does break free from his addiction of protecting his sister, will You lead him back to me? I love him. I think we could be good together. He's a strong man. He'd be a great father. And I miss him. Oh, how I miss him!

She lay back against the throw pillow and closed her eyes. She'd just keep praying. Maybe one of these days she'd wake up and her heart wouldn't be broken and she wouldn't keep wishing things had turned out differently.

"You sure you don't mind me staying here another week?" Marshall sat on one of Wade's buttery-soft leather couches in his enormous living room. A college basketball game played on the massive television.

"Stay as long as you want. It's good to have you here." Wade munched on a plate of nachos. "Sorry I wasn't around the past couple of days."

Marshall waved him off. "Don't apologize. I know you're busy."

"I've got my eye on one of the biggest pieces of land in this area. Rumor has it the owner might sell next year."

"Don't you own half the state at this point?"

"Don't I wish." He laughed.

Marshall was glad Wade had finally returned to the ranch. After two days of moping, he was awfully tired of being alone with his thoughts. Especially since they kept going back to one person.

Ainsley.

He loved her. He loved her so much he didn't know what to do with himself.

"So you gonna tell me what's really going on

with you or not?" Wade crunched a chip and leveled him with a stare.

"I told you."

"Yeah, yeah. Belle's depressed and you're letting her and Raleigh work it out. But I've never seen you like this. There's more to it."

Marshall sighed. There was more to it. A lot more. But did he want to get into the ugly details? He'd sound like a fool. Because he was a fool.

He'd let Ainsley walk out of his life. He hadn't told her he loved her.

"Well, there's this girl."

Wade lifted his eyebrows, stretched his legs out on the couch and popped another chip in his mouth. "Now we're getting somewhere."

"Ainsley. The baby nurse."

"Okay, okay. What's she look like?"

"Why?"

"So I can get a mental picture of her before I blow your socks off with my advice."

Marshall glared at him.

"What?"

"Just eat your chips."

"Fine. You never could take a joke. Tell me about her."

"Well, from the minute I spotted her, I knew she was special…" Marshall went on about how she took charge with the babies and how patient she was with Belle. He filled Wade in on how close they'd gotten, and how Belle had flipped out on them both. "And the worst thing is, Wade, I blew it. She told me she loved me. Urged me to take the job Mr. Beatty offered me in Laramie. And you know what I did?"

Wade's eyes filled with compassion. "Told her you had to stay to help Belle."

"How did you know?" He sat back, dumbfounded.

"Because you've been doing it since the day we met."

Marshall thought back on all the years since he was sent to Yearling Group Home, and his heart sank. How many events had he blown off with his best friends because he thought Belle might need him?

She hadn't even needed him most of the time. He'd just been convinced she did.

"What changed?" Wade asked.

"What makes you think anything changed?"

"You're here, aren't you?"

"Yeah."

"And you're not with Belle." He gave him a probing stare. "I didn't know the Beatty brothers were expanding. You going to take the job?"

"I haven't thought about it."

Wade swung his legs over the couch and faced him. "You haven't thought about it? Oh, man, you're in love with this Ainsley chick."

"I know."

Wade's eyes widened. "Well, what are you going to do about it?"

He shrugged. "What do you mean? I blew it. Game over."

Wade shook his head. "You've got more guts than that. The Marshall I know would walk through fire for anyone he loved."

He brightened, but slumped as quickly. "That was the old Marshall. The one obsessed with helping his sister whether she wanted it or not."

"She wanted it. She loves you."

"Yeah, well, I don't know. I feel lost. I've never…"

"Put yourself first before?"

Hearing Wade say it confirmed it was true. "Yeah."

"Did you like your old job?" Wade asked.

"You know I loved it."

"Then the first thing you should do is call Mr. Beatty and accept the job offer."

Marshall nodded.

"As for the girl, if she told you she loved you, she probably hasn't gotten over you in two days. Talk to her. Apologize. Tell her how you feel."

"When did you become Oprah?" Marshall grinned.

"I prefer Dr. Phil." He grinned back.

"I'll think about it."

"Marshall, do something for yourself for a change. You're worth it."

Ainsley's words came back: *"I'm worth more than that."* Marshall clasped his hand over his heart. She was worthy of first place. And he was worth more than putting himself second, too.

He wanted the job. He wanted to move to Laramie. And he wanted Ainsley in his life.

Now he just had to figure out how to convince her he'd changed, that he could be the man she deserved. He might have to convince himself of both, too. *Lord, I know I've done a lot of things wrong, but I need You to help me make my life right. Will You help me?*

For the first time in years, the underlying anxiety ticking inside him disappeared.

He was ready. Ready for the job. Ready for Ainsley.

"I'm sorry, Marsh."

The relief flooding Marshall almost forced him to sit on the edge of his bed. Belle had finally called him. He hadn't spoken to her since she'd thrown him out.

"How are you doing?" he asked. "How are the munchkins?"

"They're good. Raleigh took charge. He's pretty great with them…" Thick silence hung. "I went to the doctor. I didn't want to admit the awful thoughts going on in my head, but after I kicked you and Ainsley out, I realized I needed help."

"I'm glad, Belle." Hope lifted his heart.

"I'm ashamed to admit this, but every time I got near one of the babies, I thought I would hurt them. I didn't even recognize myself anymore. The doctor is treating me and recommended Raleigh and I go to counseling, and we are. It's just going to take some time."

"I'm glad you got help. You never would have hurt the babies, though." Normally, this would be the part of the conversation where he dropped everything and drove back to her house to make sure she was okay. But he didn't have the urge this time. Maybe it was the prayers or maybe he'd grown tired of feeling responsible for her. Either way, he wanted to move forward with his life. "I'm not coming back."

"I know." Her voice sounded small. "I don't expect you to. We're hiring an older widow to help with the babies in the afternoons. And, honestly, I miss you, but it's time you get back to your own life."

"I am."

"Have you talked to Ainsley?" A baby cried in the background.

"No."

"You should. I hope I didn't ruin whatever you two had."

He sighed. "You didn't ruin it, I did."

"Maybe you can fix it. I know you love her."

He smiled. He'd missed this side of her, the one who cared about him, the one who knew him better than anyone.

She continued. "I'll call her and apologize if you'll give me her number. I feel terrible about the way I treated her."

"I'm sure she'd appreciate it, but would you let me talk to her first?" He didn't want his sister meddling. This was his relationship—it was his job to deal with it.

"Okay, but I am going to apologize to her."

"I know. I'll give you her number after Christmas, okay?"

"Okay. Thank you for everything—for moving here, helping us with the babies—I don't know what we would have done without you. You're always welcome here."

"I love you, Belle."

"Love you, too. Now make things right with Ainsley."

He hung up, tapping his fingers on his phone. He intended to do just that.

Chapter Sixteen

Another Christmas Eve. Another holiday on her own.

Ainsley looked around the apartment and couldn't think of a thing she wanted to do. Tara was working until six tonight, and they planned on attending church together afterward. Until then, Ainsley had hours to fill. Yesterday, she'd called the ranchers about trying to contact her father. One of them had heard her dad was working on a sheep ranch near the Montana border. She could see him tending sheep. The rancher promised to call back as soon as he could confirm her dad's whereabouts.

Marshall hadn't called or texted either. Not that she expected him to. But every time she checked her cell, her heart would twinge, and she'd hope to see his name.

I'll get over him. Someday.

Maybe she should get a coffee. Get out of here for a while.

She went to the hall closet and found her coat. She hadn't put any makeup on and didn't care. Her hair was pulled back in a messy bun. She wound her scarf around her neck, grabbed her purse and headed to the door.

She opened it and gasped. Her purse fell out of her hands.

Marshall stood before her.

He brought a bouquet of flowers out from behind his back. "I didn't know your favorite, so I guessed."

She accepted the bouquet and buried her nose in the white roses. "They're beautiful."

He shifted from one foot to the other, gesturing to her purse. "Are you leaving? I'm not holding you up, am I?"

"I was going to the coffee shop. But it can wait."

"Are you sure?"

Her heart was beating too fast. She wouldn't jump to conclusions. Just because he was here didn't mean he'd changed his mind about staying at the ranch to help Belle or anything.

"Come in." She waved him inside, shutting the door behind him after he entered.

He took off his cowboy hat and held it in front of him with both hands.

"Have a seat." She set the flowers on the counter, then curled up on one of the chairs. He set his hat on the end table and perched on the edge of the couch.

"You were right." He looked down at his feet. "About everything. All this time I've been thinking I'm helping Belle, but all I've done is weaken her marriage. I'm ashamed to say I never gave her enough credit. I always assumed she'd fall apart if I wasn't around."

His words went down like sweet syrup. She couldn't believe he'd finally been able to see the truth about his relationship with Belle.

"After you left, it was like all the dirt and cobwebs were brushed away, and I could clearly see I needed to change. You were the catalyst, Ainsley."

She didn't want to get her hopes up. "Is that good or bad? I didn't mean to upend your entire life."

"You didn't. God did. And I'm so thankful He did. You were the biggest reason, though. I've had a lot of time to think. Last week, I let you leave without being honest with you. I let you walk out of my life, and it had nothing to do with Belle."

"What do you mean?" She braced herself. Was this the point of the conversation where he told her how glad he was they were friends and hoped she would have a nice life? Or could he possibly...love her?

"I think I've been emotionally trapped as a thirteen-year-old for years. When my mother had me sent away, I was terrified for Belle, but there was more to it."

She held her breath.

"My mother's rejection of me colored most of my actions my entire adult life."

Ainsley gasped, shocked she hadn't seen it on her own. "Oh, Marshall, I never realized how devastating that must have been for you."

He nodded. "I'd grown up wanting to believe the good guys always won and a mother's love was unconditional."

"I did, too," she said sadly.

"And I blamed myself for not being good enough, for not convincing her to dump Ed. But the other day, I finally saw her for what she was—a selfish, lonely, weak woman. And I looked in the mirror and saw the same in myself."

Ainsley crossed over to Marshall. She sat next to him, taking his hand in hers. "Don't say that. You're not selfish or weak."

"Don't kid yourself. I'm both, and until you arrived on the ranch, I had no idea how lonely I'd been." He shifted to face her. "But I want to change. I'm going to change. I have no illusions—I know I blew it with you—but I called Mr. Beatty and took the job. I told Raleigh he and Belle could work their issues out on their own. Belle actually called and apologized. She's finally getting help—you were right about everything. And I'm praying for God to help me work through my own childhood issues."

"I'm so glad," she said. "It wasn't until I began attending the Al-Anon meetings that I began healing. I'd felt so responsible and alone, and they gave me the tools to break free of my need to fix my dad."

Marshall traced his finger down her cheek. "There's more."

She shivered. Was this where he let her down? She fought the urge to turn away, to try to build a wall around her heart, but it was too late.

"I love you, Ainsley Draper. I love you, and I'm moving to Laramie, and I want to be your boyfriend and date you and explore this thing between us without all the pressure of the quadruplets and my sister."

"You want to…date me?" She blinked. He loved her? Did he really love her?

Could she handle his love? What if he reverted to his old ways? What if this was just the Christmas spirit talking?

"Among other things." He looked scared. "More than date you. I don't want to scare you off, but in my wildest dreams, we'll be married by next Christmas. In the meantime, I'll be the happiest man alive if you'll forgive me and let me see you again. I know I have a lot of trust to build with you, and I'll do it minute by minute, day by day until you have not the slightest doubt in your mind you are number one in my life."

She'd been waiting to hear those words her entire life. And this man—this good, honorable, incredible man—had finally said them. She had no reason to doubt anymore. Love was here. All she had to do was claim it.

"You are number one to me, Ainsley. You'll always be."

How could he get her to see she could trust this—could trust him? Marshall scanned her eyes for her reaction. Had he convinced her? Did she believe him?

"I want you to know I prayed about us," he said. "Watching you walk away—seeing all those gingerbread ornaments we made scattered to the wind behind your cabin—broke me. I wandered my friend Wade's ranch for a few days, and I finally got to my knees and surrendered my plans to the Lord. I know you can't possibly trust that I truly have been freed of the chains that bound me to be there for my sister, and I don't expect you to. But I will say this. It wasn't my doing. It was God's. His mercy and love set me free."

Ainsley threw her arms around his neck. "Oh, Marshall! I've been praying for you. I love you so much, and I want you to have the best life possible. This makes me so happy! We have such a good God."

"We do," he said huskily. "Does this mean you forgive me?"

She nodded, her eyes shining. "I forgive you."

Hope blossomed in his chest.

"Does this mean you're willing to date me?"

"I love you, Marshall. Love doesn't disappear in a day. I want to date you. I want to be your girlfriend. And, God willing, my wildest dreams will come true, too, and we *will* be married by next Christmas. You're the only one for me."

He crushed her to him, inhaling the scent of her shampoo and nestling his cheek into her soft hair. *Lord, thank You. Thank You! I never deserved this woman, and You blessed me with her anyway.*

"I love you, Ainsley." Leaning back, he searched her eyes. "You make order out of chaos—for the quadruplets, for Belle. And my heart—it was a disaster, but you organized it. Cleaned it out. And it's ready for you. I'm ready to give you my best."

"You helped me, too. Because you were unwilling to give up on your sister, you inspired me to reach out to my dad. Don't get me wrong, I can't go back to my old relationship with him. But I want to be in his life—even if it's simply a letter here or there."

"Would a letter be enough for you?" He pushed a lock of hair behind her ear.

She tilted her head, a hopeful smile on her lips. "For now. Maybe. I would like to hug him and tell him I love him. I want him to know I love him."

"I'll help you find him. I'll help any way I can."

"That's what I love about you, Marshall. Your heart. It's so big. So generous. You do what you say you're going to do, no matter how much it costs you. I've been looking for a man like that my whole life. My dad let me down every day. Every single day. And he said a lot of nice words, but he never followed through with them. You're not like that. You're nothing like that. And I love you."

He clung to each word, memorizing them, astounded at the healing they poured over his heart. Then he cupped her cheeks and lowered his lips to hers. The kiss sealed his future. This woman was his, and nothing could change that. He drank in her sweetness, clung to her love.

He ended the kiss, and a surge of energy infused him. He wanted to leap up and swing her in the air and run shouting through the streets.

"You're really moving here?" Ainsley asked. Her cheeks were flushed, and her eyes sparkled in wonder.

"Found an apartment yesterday."

"Where is it?"

He stood, taking her hand and leading her to the front window. He pointed to the left. "See that building? I'm two floors up. Three doors down. You can see my window from here. By the way, Dottie gave me your address."

She gasped. "You're right next door?"

"Yes, ma'am."

"This is really happening. You're moving here." She clapped her hand over her mouth and turned to him with wide, joy-filled eyes.

"I am. And I have something for you." He took out a wrapped rectangular box. "Here. Open it."

She blinked up at him, then tore off the paper. She lifted the lid off the red box and gasped. "Marshall…" With trembling fingers, she clasped the necklace. An aquamarine heart surrounded by small diamonds dangled from the silver chain. "It's even prettier than the one Dad gave me all those years ago." Tears dropped to her cheeks. "How did you know?"

"I want this to be your best Christmas ever.

Nothing bad. No flip-flop best and worst. Just the best." He put his arms around her waist.

"You've succeeded!" She threw her hands behind his neck and kissed him. He held her close, reveling in the fact she was his. This woman... He broke free of the kiss and stared into her eyes.

"You have a heart of gold, you know it, Ainsley?"

She shook her head. "No, but I like hearing you say it."

"I'll say it every day, then."

"Every single day?"

"For you? Every day wouldn't be enough. Every hour. Every minute..." He kissed her again.

She laughed. "I'll take your word for it."

"By the way, Belle is insisting she call you to apologize. You'll be getting a call from her soon."

"I like your sister when she isn't rude to me."

"I do, too." He squeezed her hand. "Now what?"

"Well, we have the entire day free. I say we get out there and enjoy it."

"Coffee first?"

"Coffee first. Come on! Let's get started!"

Epilogue

"Belle, would you get the door?" Marshall hollered to his sister in her satin baby blue dress as she exited the church.

"Of course, Marsh." She turned, grinning, as she held the church door open wide.

He swept Ainsley into his arms and carried her down to the carriage waiting for them. Everyone blew bubbles as he jostled Ainsley down the sidewalk. It was a beautiful, sunny June day. It was hard to believe he'd known Ainsley for less than a year and now they were married.

"Have I told you how beautiful you look?" He set her on the seat of the carriage and helped her arrange the train of her wedding gown.

"About fifteen times, but keep saying it. It doesn't get old." She smiled brightly at him.

He kissed the back of her hand and pressed it

against his heart. "This heart of mine is yours, you know. Forever."

"Oh, Marshall…" She let out a swoony sigh, and he tapped Jerry Cornell, Clint and Lexi's right-hand man at Rock Step Ranch, who'd insisted on driving the carriage to the Department Store, where they were holding their reception.

"You kids ready for the party?" Jerry asked, picking up the reins.

"We are."

"Well, let's giddyap." Jerry made a clicking sound to the team of Belgians pulling the carriage. "Your nuptials reminded me of the time I camped out near Yellowstone. Choked me up, I tell you. You two are like the bison…"

"Did he say we're like bison?" Ainsley whispered to Marshall.

"I believe he did." He tucked his lips under to avoid laughing. "I'm so glad you're mine."

She snuggled into his arms. The fresh air and blue skies seemed to have been ordered just for them. "Can you believe how much has changed in six short months?"

"No, I can't. Not that I had any doubt you'd get into nursing school. Two months and you'll be knee-deep in homework."

"Well, the Beatty brothers are keeping you busy." She looked up at him. "I love seeing you so happy."

"You make me happy." He pulled her closer.

"Before Christmas, I never would have thought I'd get married, let alone be blessed to have my dad walk me down the aisle. And yet, he came!"

He squeezed her shoulder. "And I had my doubts about Belle ever being motherly to the quadruplets."

After Christmas, Belle had called Ainsley and tearfully apologized. Raleigh and Belle had committed to weekly counseling sessions, and with the doctor's help, Belle had made a complete turnaround. Now she doted on the children, and Raleigh did, too. Ainsley and Marshall drove to Dushane Ranch whenever possible to see the babies.

"I know. I can't wait to hold them again. Their little tuxes and dresses are the sweetest things I've ever seen."

"You're the sweetest thing I've ever seen." He kissed her temple. The carriage turned onto Main Street and stopped in front of the Department Store. "Here we are."

Lexi and Amy crowded around them as they stepped down from the carriage. Clint and Nash held back. Tara and her boyfriend waved from the door. The only one who hadn't made it to the wedding was Wade. He had an emergency—and Marshall completely understood. Wade's closest childhood friend, a woman named Kit, was in trouble. He didn't blame Wade for missing the wedding.

They all went inside. Nash clapped him on the back. "Clint and I have been talking, and we think when Ainsley finishes nursing school, y'all should move back to Sweet Dreams. You can start your own repair shop here. What do you think?"

"I think it's your best idea yet." Ainsley stepped next to Marshall.

"You heard the lady." Marshall winked at them.

"Excuse me." A tap on Marshall's shoulder made him turn. "I wanted to thank you for taking care of my little girl."

"Of course, Mr. Draper." Marshall nodded to her father.

"You look beautiful, Ainsley." Her father was clearly fighting emotions. "Thank you for asking an old coot like me to escort you today. I don't deserve it."

Ainsley's smile broke like dawn across her face. She hugged her father. "Thank you for coming, Dad. We wanted you here. Thanks for celebrating with us."

He bowed his head. "I did you wrong…"

She touched his sleeve. "We've been over this. I forgive you. It's okay."

"You're a fine person. The best I know." He wiped under his eyes and addressed Marshall. "Take care of her. Protect her with your life."

"Gladly, sir." Marshall put his arm around her and held her to his side. "It's my life's mission."

He nodded and retreated.

"Before I take care of you and protect you, though, I want to kiss you." Marshall shifted her to face him.

"Well, time's a wasting, cowboy." She raised her eyebrows to him.

He dipped her and claimed her lips.

"Break it up, you two," Belle teased. "There are a few fellas here who want to kiss Auntie Ainsley."

Ainsley flung her hands in the air and let out a holler.

"Ben, Max. The most handsome boys I've ever seen." Ainsley took each boy out of Belle's arms. The nine-month-old twins wiggled and looked at her in wonder. She kissed each of their cheeks. "You two have gotten so big. I hope you're being good boys for your mama."

"They're the best." Belle's smile lit her face. "Oh, here come the girls."

Raleigh carried each of them. They both wore matching headbands with their dresses and ruffly tights.

"I'll take these buckaroos." Marshall lifted

Ben and Max from her arms, and she took Lila and Grace from Raleigh.

"Precious darlings." Ainsley kissed the girls' cheeks, too. "I can never get enough of your pretty faces. You look just like your mama."

"I agree. Pretty as can be." Raleigh put his arm around Belle's shoulders, and she leaned in, smiling at him. "I'm going to have to walk around with a shotgun when they get older. No one better think about messing with my girls."

Ainsley laughed. "Something tells me their big brothers will take care of them."

"Can we get a picture?" Lexi brought the photographer over. "Marshall, get closer to Ainsley, and try to get all the babies to look this way."

After several attempts, the photographer seemed satisfied. Belle and Raleigh took the quadruplets back, and Belle paused to speak to Ainsley.

"Thank you. Thank you for all your help last year, and for making Marshall so happy. I owe the babies' health to you, too. I didn't deserve to be in your wedding."

"You don't have to apologize every time you see me. We're sisters now. I love you. I couldn't imagine you not being in the wedding." Ainsley threw her arms around her and hugged her tightly. Marshall got choked up.

"You're something else, you know?" He circled his arms around her.

"I'm just…"

"Mine. And I'll thank God for the rest of my life that you said yes."

"And I'm thankful He led me to you."

* * * * *

If you enjoyed this story, pick up these other books in Jill Kemerer's Wyoming Cowboys miniseries:

The Rancher's Mistletoe Bride
Reunited with the Bull Rider

Available now from Love Inspired!

Find more great reads at www.LoveInspired.com

Dear Reader,

Babies and Christmas—two of my favorite things! When I got the idea to write about quadruplets, I pictured tiny toes, wiggly bodies and all those soft, squishy cheeks waiting to be kissed. And I also could see a mom struggling with postpartum depression and not realizing it. Marshall and Ainsley came to the rescue, but in so many ways, the babies rescued them. It's funny how life works. Sometimes tough situations lead us to clarify what we really want out of life.

This Christmas season, I hope you'll take a few minutes to bask in the beauty of God's love. He doesn't think less of us when we struggle— He sympathizes with us, loves us, wants the best for us at all times. No matter what joys or troubles the holidays bring, lean on the One who adores you—Jesus.

Have a very merry Christmas!

Jill Kemerer

Get 4 FREE REWARDS!

We'll send you 2 FREE Books
plus 2 FREE Mystery Gifts.

Love Inspired® Suspense books feature Christian characters facing challenges to their faith... and lives.

FREE
Value Over
$20